The Fifth Eye

A COLLECTION OF FICTION AND CREATIVE NONFICTION

ROISIN McLEAN

Serving House Books

The Fifth Eye:
A Collection of Fiction and Creative Nonfiction

ISBN: 978-0-9977797-0-7

Serving House Books logo by Barry Lereng Wilmont

Cover painting detail: Alexander W. Lee, American, 1907-1981
"The Law," circa 1961
Watercolor and ink, $28\frac{1}{4}$ x $36\frac{3}{4}$ in.
From the author's collection.

Cover photos, cover design, and interior design by Rosalie Herion

Published by Serving House Books, LLC
Copenhagen, Denmark and Florham Park, NJ

www.servinghousebooks.com

Member of the Independent Book Publishers Association

First Serving House Books Edition 2016

Acknowledgments and Credits

"Fisher of Herms" was first published in modified form in *Perigee: Publication for the Arts,* October 2009 (Vol. 7, Issue 2) and was reprinted in modified form in *Serving House: A Journal of Literary Arts,* Issue 10 (Fall 2014).

"Piercings" will appear in the *FDU MFA Alumni Anthology, Inaugural Issue,* forthcoming. It was a semifinalist in the 2006 Katherine Anne Porter Prize in Fiction (*Nimrod*/Hardman Awards) (in a modified version under a different pen name and title).

"The 'Sandie Five'" was first published in *OH SANDY! An Anthology of Humor for a Serious Purpose,* Lynn Beighley, AJ Fader, Andrea Donio, & Peter Barlow, Eds. (Available as a book and e-book since Mar. 2013; all profits support struggling survivors of Hurricane Sandy.) Reprinted in *Serving House: A Journal of Literary Arts,* Issue 9 (Spring 2014).

"Cleavage" was first published in modified form as "Fitted Blouse—Silk" in *Serving House: A Journal of Literary Arts,* Issue 5 (Spring 2012), and was reprinted in modified form in *Runnin' Around: The Serving House Book of Infidelity,* Thomas E. Kennedy & Walter Cummins, Eds., Serving House Books, 2014.

"White Chin Hair and the Lonely Female Cardinal" was first published in modified form in *Winter Tales II: Women on the Art of Aging,* R. A. Rycraft & Leslie What Glasser, Eds., Serving House Books, 2012, and was reprinted in modified form in *Serving House: A Journal of Literary Arts,* Issue 7 (Spring 2013).

"How Beautiful Without Shoes" was first published in modified form in *Fiction Week Literary Review,* 2011 (Spring issue), and was reprinted in modified form in *Serving House: A Journal of Literary Arts,* Issue 8 (Fall 2013).

"Dying to Dream" was first published in modified form in *Pithead Chapel: An Online Journal of Gutsy Narratives,* March 2013 (Vol. 2, Issue 3) and was reprinted in modified form in *Serving House: A Journal of Literary Arts,* Issue 8 (Fall 2013).

The epigraphs on pages 135, 136, 145, 155, 159, 160, 163, and 188 are the author's translations from Pleoneveia, *Somniare Perferre Canere Saltare,* circa 5 B.C. Every attempt was made to retain meaning, meter, rhyme scheme, and, to the extent it could be discerned, intended ambiguation.

Gratitude to Mike Smith for his reliability and generous assistance with epigraph research, and for his collegiality while working with special-needs and hard-of-hearing students.

Dedicated to Meg—joy of my life;

Steve—joy of Meg's life;

my inimitable father, Robert;

dear sweet Sir Thomas;

and Saint Walter

Contents

The Fifth Eye

PART ONE

Land and Shore

Fisher of Herms

"Correct change, sir—sorry, ma'am." The bus driver's eyes question her rugged, rectangular face and flick down past her shapeless coat to her too-dainty-for-her-height, faux-fur-trimmed boots. He coughs and hands back a rumpled dollar bill. "Ten more cents," he drones, staring at the masses on 42nd Street. Asha digs in her coat pocket for a dime—final fare from a life suffered to one she now dares to reclaim, thanks to Dr. Bida Zuglische's miracle treatment, H-lipo.

The bus strains uptown. Asha teeters and sprawls on the arm of a man so obese his massive buttocks overflow two seats. He jerks awake.

"I'm sorry!" Asha's shrill falsetto draws momentary stares. She recovers her balance, composure, and husky alto, which attracts new stares. "But thank you for—" (an arm like a king-size pillow?) "—breaking my fall."

She absorbs his appearance as his waking eyes lift to her long face and prominent brow. His striking blue eyes. His flowing, shoulder-length, silver hair. His soft, touchable lips curved in smile. His demeanor: delicate, sensitive, and effeminate, out of sync with his suit jacket, tie, and immensity. Her complete opposite. And yet—a hermaphrodite?! Seems unlikely, given the rarity. She squeezes past and unzips her coat.

She totters sideways down the aisle through pockets of Old Spice cologne, marijuana-steeped wool, curry, a phlegmy flu, dried sweat newly wet. Some passengers peer at her thick eyebrows and horsy face and wend their way down past small bosom to unzip her pants—how do city people do that? What can they learn? Truth? Brotherly love? Or fuel to fire "us against them." Oh, to flounce into a men's lav with swirls of feather boa to appall them all. But they're not worth her trouble, not anymore, not now. A pothole jolt plops her into empty seats in back. 43rd Street. The countdown begins, she thinks, but to be precise, as she always is, she must count up for uptown.

Asha settles in to wait, but migraine begins to gnaw her brain. Far above the city, she imagines, Zeus has signaled to spoil her fun and grips the bowl of her mind for lesser gods to feast. Zeus—useless and treacherous like the God of her youth. She fills her mouth with saliva, swallows two Fiorinal, and counts by thousands to 47, her age. 47th Street. How synchronistic.

Up front, the fat man suffers a sneezing attack. He needs a good pat on the back, but no one moves, so Asha does nothing. When in Rome, Greece, Manhattan. 48th Street.

Battling headache and gods in the usual way, she composes life's real-time script. Her eyes pan Manhattan through soot-dark windows. Theatre marquees spill into west 40's canyons merging east and west with sky above rivers. Gargoyles and griffins glare from Gothic cornices. Well-groomed executives shunt a bag lady in grimy plaid coat and pink bunny slippers. A disheveled man urinates on Bank of America. A vendor's black fingerless gloves conduct commerce through steam at a roasting-chestnuts cart. 57th Street.

Cradled in city movement, bus pitch, and medication, her mind drifts to the past year of wormlike food: microwaveable noodles in a cup, a steaming spaghetti test strand tossed at the wood cupboard—done, if it sticks upright; not, if it flops. Slow-motion drop of last grayed and torn bra into rainy day's waste can—go bra-less, want not. Cut to bathroom wall and a fly's faceted eyes reflecting a hundred views of a limp penis—hers. Ad nauseam, assembly-line freelance editing. Growing bank account. Close-up on checkbook and the magic number: the fee for H-lipo, new a year ago, per the website of Dr. Bida Zuglische. H-lipo manipulates a hormone, leptin, the catalyst for women's menses and menopause. An injected chemical-hormone mixture, which "Dr. Bi" does not name, reduces leptin production to a trickle. A second injection, this a chemical and amino acid combination, also unnamed, binds the remaining leptin to fat, neatly removed via liposuction. Voilá, an official adios to biological woes: true herms reborn sans "the curse" and "on-the-rag" hissy fits—sans hot flashes, night sweats, and the not-a-tickle/not-a-tingle unassaugeable aargh in the arch of each foot. Free to play at man or no-nonsense businesswoman, effective this afternoon. 63rd Street.

Asha leans her face on the cold window, away from the greasy spot, squinting in search of skyscraper tops. Dark clouds shroud the upper rooms, where gods no doubt lounge and play cat's cradle with puppet strings knotted to mortals below. 67th Street.

The final strains of the *Pastoral* overflow someone's headphones. Pleasant—Beethoven calming the final movement of female strife. Scratch that, hope dashed—hot-flash sweat pours down neck to front and backside cleavage. Asha mops with her scarf. 77th Street.

"Excuse me." Asha totters toward the front. The bus lurches right, and brakes squeal up to 78th. She fidgets behind the fat man, wedged in the aisle. He's tall.

It's early. A double espresso would be nice. Asha spots a Starbucks at the next corner and paces herself behind the lumbering fat man. Rock-salt boot droppings streak the terra-cotta tiled floor. The counter boy thinks they're together—she of the manly face and he, the feminine fat man—more of a laugh than the boy will ever know. The fat man offers to buy her espresso. Incongruous, his tenor voice and gargantuan frame. She declines and aims for a pastel armchair by the window.

"Where are you headed?" The fat man, midway back in the café, motions her to a high table, a pinhead under his girth. Her feet root between him and the comfy seat with a view.

"Uptown. An appointment." She evades the whole truth, paranoia a habit ingrained by her mother, who taught her to hide who she is because people will never understand, hide in the locker room, skip a shower after gym—better you stink than they think you have a dick.

"With Dr. Zuglische?" he asks.

"How—?" Asha mounts a bar stool at his table.

"It takes both to know both," he says with a reassuring tilt of his womanly head.

Asha scans the café, empty except for a Jackie O wannabe, with scarf and dark glasses, face in book, secluded in the back corner near a fake potted palm. Books scattered on her table.

Asha peers into his eyes, so blue. "Is that Big Apple code? You're a—hermaphrodite?"

"They call it 'intersex' now, for political correctness," he says.

"What are the odds?" she wonders aloud, brown eyes moon-sized but not yet trusting.

"This Starbucks probably sees more herms, pre or post H-lipo, than any establishment in the city," he says.

"It's a group treatment?" Asha asks in astonishment.

"No, but one person a case study does not make." He shifts for better purchase on the wooden stool.

"I'm confused. I've been saving for a year for a miraculous treatment that's strangely not front-page news, and you call it a case study?" Asha's gaze falls to his big-boned wrists, to the knuckle dimples behind each sausage finger, to the tabletop, faux marble of swirling teal to complement the café's sea-and-earth color palette.

"Our Dr. Bida Zuglische will never get government grants, and no one can benefit until trials are run. That's where we come in—we and other herms who find the H-lipo website. We are funding the next social revolution." His smile of authority reveals extraordinarily white teeth.

"What do you mean?" Asha asks, flushing at her obtuseness, her stupidity.

"Once we volunteers serve as guinea pigs to prove H-lipo works, the treatment can benefit women worldwide." His face radiates magnanimity.

All females? She's been planning for a year to become male after H-lipo. Yet another trick of Zeus and his cronies: tugging the carpet from under her carefully conceived plans.

"I suspect—with no proof, mind you—that Dr. Zuglische's goal is twofold: to sever the last shackle on women's equality, and to help herms survive. He's probably intersexed himself."

"I thought Dr. Bi was a she," Asha ventures.

"Dr. Bi. That's good. I guess his—her—gender could be perceived either way from the photo on the website. Proves the point, don't you think? In any case, the worst-case scenario if H-lipo goes awry is we get slender, svelte even, and perhaps grow wings." He winks. "If I could hide a vagina all these years, what's a pair of wings?"

Asha smiles with delight. Who could have known she'd meet a herm at all, let alone one with a sense of humor as huge as his ass?

"I'm Fat Man. Nice to meet you." He reaches to shake her hand.

"You're not fat," Asha lies. "Fat is leaving your home in a piano crate."

"You are a kind liar," Fat Man says. His smiling eyes are tropical blue. Not fake contact-lens blue. True Caribbean Sea blue. His protective grasp envelops her small-boned hand.

Asha considers names. Sebastian won't do. "Chimera. Pleased to meet you."

He opens the first of two bottles of Fiji water lined up between them.

"Cheers! How'd you get here?" Fat Man asks.

Unused to conversation, Asha fumbles, "Do you mean in life or today?"

"Take your pick," Fat Man says.

"Given the way my brain compartmentalizes, the story begins at age 12." She checks her watch. "It's eleven—my appointment's at one o'clock—here's the abridged version."

"Mine's at noon. Fire away." Fat Man settles in, clasps his hands comfortably between sagging breasts and belly shelf.

Don't fall for comfort and familiarity, her mother always said. Never drop your guard, her mother says in her head.

"Since my first menstruation" (Mother dear-est, drop dead), "I've used 'red H's' to describe a *Host* of dilemmas—H for *Hormones, Herms,* etc." She exhales her H's like breath in frosty air. "I discovered my first flow with *Horror* one summer at dawn as I squatted over a pee *Hole* in the ground on an overnight *Hike* two miles down a *Hill* from local *Hygiene.* An inauspicious welcome to woman*Hood.* Back then, you *Had* to endure menstrual cramps. The school nurse, '*Helms* from *Hell,*' tsk-tsked at my suffer-ing so I *Heaved* on her desk. The next month, she pointed straightaway to the bathroom, and I *Hurled* while closing the door. Puke gushed around the frame, in and out, lovely sight. But I digress."

Fat Man grimaces and laughs. "You had it bad!" He unscrews the blue cap of the second Fiji bottle.

Behind Fat Man, college students fling backpacks beside lounge chairs, chairs too small for Fat Man's rump, which hangs off his stool and draws rolling eyes from the stu-dents. Fat Man excuses himself, buys two more Fijis for him and another espresso for her.

"You read my mind, thank you." Asha continues in a quieter tone. "The night sweats started— Is this too much information?"

"Your history is uniquely yours yet affirms normalcy in mine. Please continue," Fat Man says.

They contemplate each other. Few people understand. Few herms ever meet.

She disentangles the silver earrings from her brunette mane. "The night sweats started four years ago. The periods stopped, but not the hot flashes. Screaming 'Why me?' at the ceiling proved futile."

Fat Man rubs his belly like a marine biologist wets down a beached whale. "Yup, been there. So I decided to travel. Lived in an RV, which amazingly shrank. RV this big, me—" His hands spread wide. His honesty is a magnet; his voice, a compass. "Finally settled in a roomy log cabin out west. You?"

"I searched for relief online. I didn't trust men to find a cure, so I explored only sites that mentioned female doctors, which meant interminable clicking, two steps back, one step forward." Asha taps the table with her index finger.

Fat Man teases: "Don't think I didn't hear that streak of feminism."

Asha smiles paternally through her Freud impersonation: "Men vahnt vomen zubzervient, zlavess to their bodiss, number two in a patriarchal zoziety. Thiz iss vell-known fact."

As Fat Man laughs, his belly shakes like a hiccuping Shamu, like a sloshing water balloon flung from upper rooms.

"Number two as in shit," Asha adds.

"I got there. Are you an actor, Chimera?" Still laughing, he drapes his jacket on a nearby chair, then wipes his neck and face with a clean napkin.

Asha does the same. Can it be that their hot flashes come at the same time? "I'm a copyeditor by trade, romance novels, arcane university-press manuscripts, the gamut. But I'm a director at heart—I like the control."

Fat Man's eyes light anew on her face, not like the gripping migraine now past.

"You were raised boy," Asha says.

"Yes." Fat Man gazes into middle space and memory, then smiles. "I grew to love words and context. *Cast, pearl, slip, and seine?* Father teaching fishing. *Cast, purl, slip, and skein?* Mother teaching knitting."

"So you were *cast* in a dual role," Asha adds slyly.

Fat Man's eyes crinkle with appreciation. "No, but Mother did insist on planting seeds of choice."

Asha ducks and whispers, "I think the kids at that table are eavesdropping." She nods subtly in their direction.

Fat Man glances over his shoulder. "They're harmless. Too impressed with their navels to bother with old farts."

"Thanks so much." Asha feigns offense but can't help grinning.

"You were raised girl," Fat Man states.

"Yes, and I'm female at the core." Asha sighs. "But I've been planning on switching to celibate man."

Fat Man scrutinizes her face and finds no answer. "Why?"

"Because I never—. It doesn't—. To provide for the future. I can die an old male content in my own digs with untapped money in my bank account, or an old female who outlives her savings and lands in the state nursing home fending off fondlers. I have to play man—it's as simple as math."

"Have to? Math? Where is the honesty, humanity, in that?" Fat Man asks with concern.

"Herms and humanity? Oil and water." That said, she hears her own negativity, preached to one who seems to perceive more than she. "Let's change the subject."

"Why?" Fat Man asks in earnest, not to provoke.

She confides with sadness, "So I don't get—ugly-er."

He reaches verbally to console her. "'Beauty lies in the eye of the beholder.' Beauty lies."

Asha nods without assimilating fully. Silence menaces their conversation, the honest kind, which strangers share when they don't expect to meet again.

He prompts with her earlier comment: "So you followed web links to hermaphroditism?"

"Yes. Herms—the cruelest prank ever played by the gods." Asha's displeasure pinches her lips, flares her nostrils.

"Gods plural?" he asks.

"A drunken clique contriving our pitfalls for perverse amusement. One deity would never abuse his children this way." She searches his lips for a sign of agreement.

"Define 'way'," Fat Man says. His arms rest on the table like felled masts. Her slender hands, placed near his, tingle. Her arm hair rises, concealed under long, pewter-gray sleeves.

She can't fathom his need for explanation. "The way the world sees us: as freaks."

"The world doesn't know who we are unless we tell them. I don't see myself as a freak. But, I agree, the world is hermaphobic." Fat Man nods, then adds, "We all have phobic stereotypes."

"I don't." Asha gasps—too-quick a response, denial exposed.

"Are you sure?" His eyebrows arch.

She studies the table. Fat people wallow in their own waists. Their drooping buttocks? Proof of rebuttals to self-control. But, in all fairness, Fat Man seems noble, no glutton, no bull.

"Once we grant ourselves permission, we can love them as ourselves, love ourselves through them," Fat Man suggests.

Asha frowns. "How Christian."

"I am Christian." He pulls a silver cross and chain from inside his blue shirt.

She projectile-vomits words at his face, "If we're made in God's image, did Jesus have a vagina?!"

Conversation stops at the college kids' table. The counter boy, on tiptoe, peeks over cup stacks. The Jackie O wannabe could be from Madame Tussaud's. Asha grapples fast for a feasible explanation, finds it, fills the silence with a stage whisper: "You know, the line from *The Vagina Monologues*." Nearby conversation resumes.

"Brilliant cover," Fat Man whispers. He excuses himself and heads for the restrooms. Out of sight of the others, he catches Asha's eye. He points to the Men's Room door, scratches his head in puzzlement, squeezes into the Women's Room. Asha laughs so hard she almost pees. Fat Man returns, breathing heavily. The stool complains under his weight.

"How often do you do *that?*" Asha asks, still convulsed with delight.

"Whenever someone needs a laugh," Fat Man says with kindness.

"Thank you, and please forgive my outburst." Asha smiles in embarrassment and whispers, "I truly am curious, though—Do you believe Jesus had a vagina?"

Fat Man's instant response: "If He did, do you trust he could understand you, love you?"

An unsettling question. She recalls the initial warmth of her Sunday school teacher. The nasty boy under the table sticking his hand up her skirt and fingering her underpants. His giggling. The teacher doing nothing about it. No scolding. No nothing, except the word spreading into taunts and conspiratorial grins. Outcast in God's house. Her mouth opens. No words form.

Fat Man leans close. "Let's make it more tangible. I am a man, and I have a vagina—ambiguous and dysfunctional, mind you, but a vagina nonetheless. Do you think I could understand you, love you?"

"Yes." She holds her breath.

Their eyes lock. "There's your answer." He leans back and pounds the table like a judge's gavel. The students glance over but continue talking.

"Fundamentalists would burn you at the stake," Asha whispers, intrigued. His silver hair gleams like angora in the sun. "Do you have a significant other?" She ponders her brave words, new and satisfying.

"I'm not partnered, but I've attracted a chubby chaser or two." He winks.

She tries not to laugh at her image of him on top, a limbed ton of granite deflating his lover's lungs. He drains the fourth Fiji, which seeps from his skin in armpit sweat rings.

Dare she ask? Yes, it's logical. "You'll stay male after H-lipo?"

"No."

Asha runs her fingers around the espresso cup rim. "If God made us in his image, why do you want to change?"

"Call it an exercise in free will," Fat Man says.

Too cryptic. Her face drops. Although, if she adopts a male persona, and he female, there is still a chance for—commingling. "I like your eyes," she says before thinking.

"I like your eyes, too," says Fat Man, quietly, which, just like that, sets Asha's body on fire. She tries to keep surprise and "love me, for God's sake, please" off her face. God singular?

"I want to explore myself and female voice," Fat Man explains. "I'm a writer. Lover of words, symbols, and myth. Technical writer by day, mostly software manuals, lucrative contracts. Fiction writer by night."

"A writer," she repeats. Titillation of the mind is a magnificent turn-on.

Fat Man's curiosity, Bunsen burner blue in each iris, crests in waves that wash through her eyes and down, to pool warm down there, lapping against and in. Fiction by night. Fusion by candlelight. Asha's modesty slips to her ankles under his visual probe, which tongues and sucks in tantalizing foreplay. Her code of celibacy yields like a virgin's hymen.

"There are other ways," Fat Man says.

"Ways to what?" asks Asha, wide-eyed, fearful he refers to the *Kama Sutra,* which she's never read.

"Ways to study female voice and myself. But H-lipo will be faster. Once leptin is removed, at least this once, I hope to assess what doesn't feel 'normal' or what does, assuming the answer's in the contrast. Time will tell."

"How long?" Asha asks. The passion she'd sought futilely for so long, and finally spurned, now burns in throat, virgin's vagina, and penis-size clitoris afire with desire but lifeless, superfluous. She could part her legs under the table and grasp him tight, again and again while enfolded in his massiveness, filled, embraced by the filler, merging—a dream of lust masquerading as love in the dreamer's eye. Lust lies in the eye of the beholder. Lust lies.

Fat Man whispers, "Long enough to prove who I am."

Asha swims nude in his eyes, lapis lazuli and turquoise in a Caribbean inlet. In let. Let in. Leptin. Sirens slice the air, and red lights blip across Starbucks' walls. The fake Jackie O stares at her page.

"Where have you been all my life?" Asha winces at her boldness and the worn cliché.

"Mostly traveling. Home is Parks, a tiny town between the Grand Canyon and Flagstaff. You?"

"Home is Pomona, Pennsylvania, between the Poconos and coal country."

Fat Man smiles. "Pomona, goddess of abundance—horns of plenty! Our P's, your H's—pH, alkaline and acid, balanced. Could be a sign."

Asha shrugs, suddenly shy. "Only that we're both and neither. In between." The sheets. Is there a back room here? No time.

"May we exchange emails?" Fat Man writes his address on a napkin.

She pulls a notepad from her purse, prints neatly, glances at her watch. "Time for you to go." Stool legs scrape.

"Give me a hug, Chimera, my new friend," Fat Man says, opening his arms wide.

"Call me Asha." She presses her breasts into his. His arms envelop her like a plumped goose down quilt. Despite the rotunda of his abdomen, impressive arousal lower down. He'll feel no movement in her down there, not that kind. His question answered? His sweat rings have no smell. Does he like her jasmine scent?

"Call me Simon. After H-lipo, let's meet downtown at the TKTS kiosk, 47th and Broadway. Six o'clock? I'll get tickets for *Phantom of the Opera.* We'll go out for dinner first. My treat." Fat Man holds her coat just so, and she slips her arms easily into the sleeves as though they'd perfected the act over years.

"I'm dying to see it," Asha says. "But I'd miss my bus home."

"I'm staying downtown in Tribeca, at a B&B with some vacancies. It's safe." Fat Man's assurance is matter-of-fact. "All spacious rooms complete with toiletries. A gourmet breakfast: eggs Benedict, crêpes with sour cream, fresh cantaloupe with berries."

"We'll make a night of it!" That's not what she means! Or is it? "I mean—" Falsetto voice again.

"'Make your choice'," he says sternly, then breaks into a grin. "A line from *Phantom.* There's no pressure, Asha. I'm as comfortable with you as alone."

She lowers her eyes to hide her disappointment.

"And that's as comfortable as anyone can ever be." His voice soothes, and his hand presses lightly against the small of her back in gentlemanly guidance toward the door. His touch rekindles fire. Asha conceives the script fast: Thrust him back on the stool and straddle him tight, unbuckle his belt as he raises her skirt, his immense paunch an impenetrable wall that blocks what she seeks, his redwoodian manhood. Her pelvic bones stretch; fine fractures permit a full ten centimeters. Cut! She's seeking *her* manhood (right?), not his, not giving birth. Brakes screech over on Broadway. He'll burn for blasphemy, she for fickleness and lust.

"Why don't you go ahead, Simon." Asha nods at the door. "I've got to see a woman about a horse."

He squeezes her hand tenderly, says, "Let go, let God," and kisses her smack on top of the head where it is soft during infancy until the skull fuses.

Around the corner, en route uptown, he passes the café windows. Pausing, he peers in and salutes, then waddles from view, all four hundred pounds of him. The college students mimic waddling in their chairs but seem genuinely embarrassed when they realize she's watching.

She heads for the restroom. On the tiled wall over the sink, the spell breaks as surely as if mirror shards flew. Too old for romantic nonsense, too set in her ways. For a year, driven by one goal with a lifetime of reasons. Plan A never needed a letter before, yet its rationale can't hold a candle to passion; Plan B, an adolescent dream of requited love. H-lipo changes hormones. Will she still be *her*, afterward? Should she risk a death of sorts to live, or risk a life of sorts to love? Why does desire confuse the issue at the eleventh hour?

The students are gone. She stops by Jackie O—clever, up close, how lifelike the mannequin's hands. Some joker has turned her book upside down. The purple stripe on the side seems oddly provocative; purple is her favorite color. "Read and Share," says a sign by the scattered books. Asha removes the thick paperback, *Kerrigan's Copenhagen,* tucks it into her purse, and props a different book in the motionless hands.

Each step uptown toward Dr. Bi's clinic confuses Asha further until she stops, too unsure to proceed, her boots inside large shoe prints on a dusting of snow. A downtown bus strains to the curb. Its door hisses open. She mounts the steps on shaking legs and sinks to a seat. Fingering the white napkin with Fat Man's—Simon's—contact info, she watches the city slip by her window. Snow settles and melts on subway-heated sidewalks, coats people like confectioners' sugar. Their heads hang penitent before wind-flung flakes. Humanity, fallen from grace? Snow falls from the heavens, from grace, on all of God's diverse children, yes? Simon's napkin doesn't answer.

A woman behind her reads aloud in a Southern drawl. "Central Park is itself a work of art, including 80 statues and monuments. Artists Christo and Jeanne-Claude's *The Gates*—7,500 saffron banners, free-hanging from saffron vinyl frames—is free to the public and open February 12th through 28th. Viewed from buildings surrounding the park, the closely spaced banners simulate a golden river winding through leafless branches, highlighting 23 miles of pedestrian paths." [1]

Restless, bewildered, she gets off the bus at 72nd, dons scarf and dark glasses against brilliant snow. Eastward lie open gates crowned with saffron banners, which billow with chill breeze and beckon like ritual to wandering pilgrims. She walks toward and among playful throngs, following snowy footpaths festooned with sunny orange. Engrossed, she stops below frenetic yet frozen bronze wings—the "Eagles and Prey" statue. Horns of a dilemma: a snow-coated woolly goat is wedged in a cleft, between a rock and a hard place; an eagle's talon pierces the fearful dying goat like a liposuction hose.

Further east to "Christopher Columbus," bold explorer, who gazes heavenward with outstretched arm, palm raised. Amid those gathered at the statue, a father reads to his blind teenage daughter, whose long chestnut hair flies free on the wind: "scoffed at before,/ during the voyage, menaced,/ after it, chained,/ as generous as oppressed,/ to the world he gave a world." [2]

---

[1] The quotation, "Central Park is itself a work of art..." is from a New York City press release dated 22 January 2003: "Mayor Michael R. Bloomberg Announces Agreement with Artists Christo & Jeanne-Claude for 'The Gates' in Central Park."

[2] Full text, in English and Italian, of the inscription from the statue of Christopher Columbus appears online at: Central Park: Columbus Monument.

The teen smiles and catches snowflakes on her tongue. Church bells flood the changing wind with a hymn from Asha's youth, "Holy, Holy, Holy." She heads south toward their peal. "There is none beside Thee," the blind girl sings in as pure a soprano as a Vienna Choirboy. Asha turns. The girl smiles through her as at a distant steeple.

Orange banners flap and swirl like matador capes, guiding Asha toward the bells—toward transportation home or TKTS kiosk. Past South American "El Libertador," Simon Bolivar, whose breathless steed, petrified in bronze, stands transfixed pawing air above a boiling saffron sea. Liberator. Simon. Lover of words, symbols, and myth. Simon, "Fisher of Herms." He will like that, even after H-lipo. She pulls notepad from purse and prints, "Buy underwear." Hanes, she wonders, pen in air? She pictures her usual plain-Jane white cotton. "*Hardly*." The lone word gusts with her breath and disappears. She writes in cursive on the pad, and her words billow and dance on the wind, "*Heliotrope* satin." Ice crystals fall, frozen in perfection for an infinite second, melt, and bleed her inked words.

Piercings

Behind him, the door latched shut with a heavy *chuck-click,* and before his knapsack hit the floor, First Lieutenant Stefan Forrest spun around in a crouch with an invisible M16A2. Get a grip, he thought, and straightened to six-five, then stooped to the peephole just to be sure. Satisfied with the all-clear, he picked up the Soldier's Angels' transitional knapsack and threw it to the hotel's floral peach and moss spread, the seams of which did not match properly, peony to peony, iris to iris, as they should.

His Deaf mother, a tailor, devoted impeccable attention to such visual detail, a trait that had informed his senses, his way of thinking, of being. If she were here, she would shake her head and sign large about the spread's example of productivity-crazed sloppiness. He imagined a bonfire-sized heap of limp and ragged quilting scraps with petrified body parts sticking out at all angles—yet another prickly image of past confronting present. Or present skewering the past. Hard to tell which took precedence. All he really needed was—. Was what? A good long dose of oblivion, he guessed.

He lay down beside the bed, clasped his hands under the black stubble of his buzz-cut skull, and assessed the situation while his eyes traced crescent swirls in the white stucco ceiling. Honorably discharged, almost home, and free. As free as any soldier back on U.S. soil who has learned the price. Which started the roller coaster ride from the trenches of his mind spiraling down to his bowels, where he, a shit-faced homunculus, hid from himself.

Survivor guilt gurgled in his windpipe with a snore. Soaked in fear, he awoke with a jerk half under the bed and bashed his forehead on the metal frame—hard proof that the weight of Carl's headless body, splayed akimbo, was not trapping his legs, flooding him in blood. Moose wasn't there either, dragging him to safety, with canines gentle yet firm on his arm. The box spring smelled of chemicals and dust, and a violent sneeze banged his head again in the casket-close space. Panting, he thrust his head under the bedspread out to fresh cooler air. Twilight filtered through drapes wafting in breeze at the window. He recited his mantras. First, mind over body. Second, mind over brain—bizarre, he knew, but ever since he'd surfaced from oblivion at 212th MASH near Najaf, a transparent silver curtain had encased his brain like a cozy body bag, disconnecting "him" from his now former "self," and everything changed.

His pulse and breathing gradually slowed. Moose, his chocolate lab back home, couldn't have been here anyhow. Stefan tried to sense her in his mind. Her velvet-soft ears. Her intelligent, gold-flecked eyes ascertaining his mood. Her tail thumping in a happy wag as she slept. The smell of fresh-mown grass on the pads of her paws even in winter. He tried to picture her, but her image rippled like desert heat.

Nearby machine roar clenched his gut. He wrested his legs free of the bed, sprang between it and the door, and twisted back and forth to gauge the whereabouts of the enemy, his good ear still learning to work alone. He flung the door open so hard it crashed into the wall and scared the daylights out of a pony-tailed maid steering a vacuum past his room. Too frightened to scream, she fled down the hall.

"Sorry," Stefan called as she ran behind the vacuum, which careened and lurched until it banged into the wall, fell over, and blocked the hall. She leapt the noisy machine in a glorious stride and disappeared through a stairwell door.

An undeniably menacing figure, Stefan noticed, blocked the light spilling from his room to the dim hallway. And the shadow, of course, didn't show his whole story.

He shut the door and didn't startle at the *chuck-click* this time. He sat on the bed, folded his hands in his lap, and waited for the MPs. Not MPs, he corrected himself, hotel security guards.

Minutes passed. The vacuum roar stopped. No knock on the door. No sound.

He bounced on the mattress—the yielding of it a middle ground in time. Behind him, sandbags, cots, and hospital beds. Ahead, his comfy, king-size bed at home, an extra long so his feet fit. Home. He sank his face into his hands, felt the cleft in his cheek, the throbbing egg on his forehead.

Mind over brain. Everything would be OK at home. Family. Church. Interpreting in sign language for the Deaf congregation in the front right pews—his mom, Aunt Sydney, and their long-time Deaf-school friends. As with Moose, their images wavered, a blur of signing hands.

The congregation would be proud of him, of course. At least on the surface. Had they prayed for his kills? Or would the kills make them shun him now? What on earth could he say to them? My name is Stefan, I'm a murderer, haven't a clue what "right thinking" means, and "Semper Fi"? "Right-wing Christian" and "righteous pacifist" had become twisted rhetoric now that Iraq had torn him to shreds. Maybe it would make sense by Sunday. What day was it anyway? His head pounded. He touched the bump on his forehead and checked his fingers. No blood.

In the fluorescent-lit bathroom, he downed three glasses of cold water and peered at his face. A lunar landscape. Right temple with burgeoning purple-crested lump. Cavernous blue-gray eyes. High cheekbones. Shrapnel crater in left cheek. Dimples, which after thirty years still looked boyish rather than Marlboro Man rugged. Fear's pallor had drained his skin of its desert tan. Funny. He didn't feel afraid just now; it was only a nightmare. Only? Only recurring torturous memories that he both did and did not want to forget. He must remember and honor the dead, no matter what.

A shower would help. He twisted the silver-link watch over his knuckles and curled it behind the chrome faucet on the sink. After he stripped, he lost his balance—not uncommon when the hearing goes, he had learned—and landed on the toilet, where he sat for a while, elbow on knee, imagining himself as Rodin's "Thinker" holding a cold wet washcloth to his fiery forehead. The throbbing marched to the beat of his pulse, like bursts from his rifle, without which he still felt vulnerable to the crosshairs of another.

The ceramic floor tiles, cold on the soles of his feet, reminded him of the two-day autumn between summer and winter over there—the dusty, bloody world across the sea. Stefan reached for the bath mat draped on the tub, whose white porcelain shone like the sunny smiles of Sunni children. They mass when he flashes packs of Chiclets, some shy at first but then friendly compatriots practicing salutes and marching *hup* until *parade rest.* Their hair is the same color as his, so dark the highlights shine blue in the sun.

He couldn't reach the mat, so he stood and stretched for it, dropped it to the floor, raised the toilet seat lid, sat again.

He tried to piss until it hurt, but nothing happened. No news flash there. Landstuhl nurses were forever *tsk-tsk'*ing at his teaspoon's worth in the damn bedpan. He had strained so hard to merit their good graces he produced hemorrhoids instead of one-and-a-half liter's daily urine.

Without rising, he turned the sink spigot and listened to the water. When that didn't work, he closed his eyes and pictured the bathroom back home. His Deaf mom had researched how to accommodate his hearing and bought a framed photo of Niagara Falls, which she hung at his toddler eye level when he sat on the "throne." All that, when she couldn't even hear water running, didn't know it made sound, couldn't know what sound was.

He wept without tears. All he wanted in the world was her. And an hour of boredom. And to piss in peace. Carl can't piss anymore, so why should I, Stefan asked of no one because he knew the doctors' answer: it was all in his head. A head full of piss. Shit for brains. Welcome home.

Swaddled by steam in the shower, he got a crazy idea, too impulsive to justify, and it excited him in a way he had no choice but to indulge. He rushed to towel off and dress in white civvies, which he must stop calling civvies because now they were, as before—how long ago?—simply clothes. The cover of the phone book tore as he dislodged it from the drawer of the walnut-veneer desk. Running his index finger down the "Body Piercing" column in the Yellow Pages, he stopped short: no chalky desert dust coated his hand. He basked in cleanliness until a sense of inner filth erupted in his gut. His index finger rested on a large ad for an APP-approved studio called "Wild Will's." Probably swarming with anti-war youth, so slouched in their cup of apathy they couldn't see past the rim. What with his military posture still branding him a soldier, they'd probably smirk in their self-righteous fashion. Or stare at his neck, no longer ramrod straight. No matter—he was set on this crazy idea, and there'd be plenty of time to rationalize it later.

Along the walls of Wild Will's studio, chrome-framed photos and mirrors reflected superimposed views: cars on the street and a kaleidoscope of gems on rotating carousels—ruby, Volvo, emerald, Honda, topaz, Camry, sapphire, Lexus. The place felt right, and Stefan smiled, soothed by the colors of Christmas tree lights and of stained-glass windows backlit with sun. The absence of other customers suited him fine.

Alcohol tinged the air in the antiseptic back corner. White cartons emblazoned with red type lined the counter—STERILE gauze prep wipes, STERILE capped syringes, and STERILE latex gloves—with a white BIOHAZARD on a bright blue canister for used needles. The padded chair felt comfortable with its adjustable headrest, but Wild Will, a Nam vet—"once a soldier, always a vet, and we vets hang together forever, y'know"—insisted on jerry-rigging some towels to support Stefan's neck. A useless gesture—his neck was fused there—but he let Will do the fellow-vet thing. Will's appearance inspired partial confidence: meticulously clean, well-groomed fingernails; flabby triceps; and a gray wispy beard sporting different kinds of crumbs.

"Ready? This will hurt a bit," Will warned as he leaned in to begin.

No shit, Stefan thought, but he kept his mouth shut—best not to insult a vet with a needle in his hand. Stefan closed his eyes and pondered the irony of his decision, which is when he understood how really crazy it was: paying to insert metal into flesh from which shrapnel had been removed. Smooth—sharp. Choice—force. Peace—war. Holy War—what a fucking oxymoron.

Too angry to want to believe in God anymore—thanks to 9/11, Iraq, and now this curtain around his brain that effectively sealed him off from himself, the Marines, and the rest of the world—he refused to give up on Christ. One helluva conundrum, believing in the prophet but not the god. A god who chose not to intercede when the powerful elite garbled their secular agenda: Holy Oil. Our Father, who art in Humvee, hallowed be thy frame, thy pistons hum, thy war be won, red Ford, blue Plymouth, black Lincoln.

"So?" Will asked, handing Stefan a mirror.

Stefan jumped. Once again, he'd taken a mental powder.

He forgot and tried to lift his neck, which of course wouldn't yield, then lowered and angled the mirror to check that Will had followed his specifications.

Three garnets paralleled the curve of his right ear lobe, like three stars in the Islamic crescent that proclaimed to the heavens every mosque dome and minaret, so he could honor each of the righteous-eyed lives he'd taken with 30-round bursts from his M16—three young lives, barely teens. Down the rubble-strewn street, two writhe, shriek Arabic—at him or for mother or Allah?—and finally slump against each other, still, silent, as silent as the blood pooling beneath them. Nearby, in the doorway of a pitted stone house, a twitching third lies on his side, his long black curls in a whorl around his head. The boy's astonished gaze shifts from the AK47 on his fingerless palm to Stefan's approaching boots, ankle-deep in dust, and then up to Stefan's eyes, where the gaze fixes forever, life gone, just like that. The tingling starts in Stefan's soles and rises, a systemic peristaltic wave that soon vibrates his knees, his hands, and the M16. It numbs his cheeks and clamps a lead skullcap to his brain, which strains to flee, can't, and replays the scene in visual dry heaves because his eyes are impaled on the dead boy's gaze.

"Can you see OK?" Wild Will asked.

Stefan shifted the mirror. Gracing the curve of each nostril were two steel beads, one for Juan, one for Denzel. Leading the convoy into Najaf, Denzel's truck trips an IED and explodes. His arm with the "Ma" tattoo, severed at the shoulder and flung with the truck door, slams into Stefan's bulletproof windshield, which crumples into accordion pleats of tie-dyed red and camo green.

"Hey, you OK?" Will asked, ducking to see into Stefan's eyes. A crumb dropped from his beard onto Stefan's white trousers.

Stefan nodded. Battery B, 3rd Battalion, 104th Field Artillery. Good men. But they're jumpy and learn fast to distrust all Iraqis, all Muslims. Stefan objects in principle but can't blame his men and doesn't try to dissuade them; their lives there depend on their misplaced hate.

"Stay put. I've got just the thing," Will said, gesturing to the back of the studio as he rose.

Stefan brushed the crumb from his thigh and tilted the mirror. A steel bead ring, a circle of friendship, pierced his right eyebrow to honor Carl, a South Jersey farm boy who looks up to him as to a surrogate father. Carl's headless body props for an infinite second on the turret gun, a silhouette bleeding on a yellow sky. His torso and wobbly scarecrow limbs collapse in slow motion onto Stefan. The fall of body and darkness. The explosion in Stefan's neck and ear, when sticky, salty warmth floods his face, runs up his nose and down his throat, and he doesn't know if he's choking on Carl's blood or his own. The pall of half-heard whispers at 212th MASH near Najaf, whispers that didn't stop in Landstuhl and won't now or ever.

Stefan swung the mirror to his left. Bizarre, a deafened ear with tinnitus. His deaf ear heard ringing—sometimes exasperating beyond comprehension, sometimes soothing like the cosmos humming. Sometimes it didn't ring at all. In the lobe of the deaf ear, a clear crystal now shone, a talisman of hope rooted in his flesh in honor of his mom and Aunt Syd's think-positive, can-do ethic. Would they feel blessed he's now half-deaf? Long accustomed to drifting between cultures, between the hearing and deaf worlds, Stefan knew he was now being torn apart—between Iraq and home, desert and river, past and present, faith and doubt. Lost, lost, and still not found.

Will returned with a manila folder. "Chicks go wild, dude, over piercings on the glans." His salacious grin revealed a large silver bead in the middle of his tongue. And surprisingly small teeth, like those of the young Shiites, giggling and scrambling for Fritos and Oreos. Their skin is olive-bronze, a shade darker than Stefan's.

"Just the thing you need," Will said. He took the mirror and handed Stefan the folder, opened to His and Her photos of turquoise-studded genitalia. Will's bald spot shone as he hunched near-sighted over the upside-down photos and admired his handiwork—or perhaps the excited genitalia, if his flushing pate was a clue. If studding your prick wasn't crazy, Stefan didn't know what was. And with that involuntary disgust came the clarity of stadium lights blazing on night sky: his intuitive rationale for getting pierced was to honor the fallen on both sides of the war, to rebel against the authority which made him a party to it, and to respect his lifeline, his Deaf family's innate hope. All of which stood befouled by these studded pricks and clits. Whatever happened to monogrammed towels? Stefan wondered, feeling prudish and old, older than Will, older than Queen Victoria, a joke of a Marine. The kids shouldn't see this—. Mind over brain. Home.

Stefan shoved the folder away and grabbed a wad of bills from his wallet. He hardly listened to Will's aftercare instructions about H_2Ocean, a can of saltwater spray. Stefan shoved the can in a pants pocket with the receipt.

"And—this is important—to avoid bacterial infection, no swimming for six weeks!"

Stefan smiled at the jingle of bells on the door, the breeze on his face. Just a few hours more, and he'd be home.

The southbound bus lulled him to sleep. When he awoke by the window, the aisle seat held only a *People* magazine. Stefan couldn't remember a seatmate. It was a blank—another split suture exposing the curtain for what it was: an alien patchwork of BEFORE stitched to the unthinkable IN-BETWEEN, awaiting shapeless swatches of the YET-TO-COME. The shrinks at Landstuhl diagnosed the curtain as a defense mechanism, but Stefan was convinced it had mutated like a virus, filtering reality and even childhood memories through Iraq. His gut told him not to tell the shrinks that. He bluffed and told them what he sensed they wanted to hear—"Yes, indeed, a miracle I knew sign language *before* becoming deaf." Incredibly, they bought his absurd statement and sent him home without PTSD penned on his chart.

His swollen bladder stabbed a knife stroke of pain through his gut, and a deep voice on the other side of the curtain said *blah-blah-blah pit stop.* Stefan lurched and banged his forehead into thick windowpane. His arms were hugging his shins, with his knees tucked up under his chin. Pain and panic collided in his mind. Was he really here on this bus? Or was he comatose in Landstuhl, this trip his life's reprise as his lungs filled with piss? Were these the death throes of memory? Why mask horror with horror? Wait—masking death throes was an act of compassion, not evil. Was the curtain God? Round and round, and back to ground zero. Stefan's head ached so bad he wished it would explode. Passengers peeked and stared and gave him a wide berth as they piled off the bus to stretch their legs.

Mind over body. Mind over brain. He trailed the bus driver into a Wawa convenience store. Stefan liked Wawa's; there was one back home. Everything would be OK at home. Newspapers lined the storefront racks: *Asbury Park Press, Ocean County Observer.* The words floated out of reach, wouldn't process into meaning. He grabbed a box of Excedrin Migraine and joined the driver at the coffee machine.

"What state are we in?" Stefan asked.

The bus driver spoke through a yawn. "The Pope says a state of grace." He chuckled at his wit and passed Stefan the carafe.

Pennsylvania? Kansas! "Pardon?" Stefan leaned closer with his good ear and poured rich Colombian Dark Roast into a small cup.

"New Joisey. Garden State. Take your time, Joe. I gotta see a man about a horse."

Stefan looked around, wondering what era and bathroom the driver had in mind. He noticed out the window part of a sign not obscured by the bus: "—aghan's Liquors." Monaghan's Liquors? Only then did Stefan recognize the store, *his* Wawa, *his* Route 37 outside. The joy that surged through his chest slammed to a stop, imploded into shame. The unexpected shock of it made him dizzy.

It took several tries to get the carafe back in the rimmed base. Stefan gripped the countertop. This wasn't right. He'd lain tense in traction week after week fearing separation of head and body, recovered from surgery to fuse cervical vertebrae, and shared pride with ward mates for serving their country. With great ceremony, the commander had pinned Purple Hearts to their hospital gowns, everyone's but Stefan's. Not to worry, just a paperwork snafu; it would come after he was stateside. A blessing in disguise—without an award, he could pretend Iraq never happened. But it had, and here he was, and what the hell was wrong with him? How could he be unworthy of home? He reached for his piercings to be sure they were there. Under the crystal of hope, the lobe of his deaf ear burned hot and sore.

The bus driver left, disappearing around the corner, no doubt looking for a private wall behind the store. Stefan glanced at the fisheye mirror over the counter and met the eyes of a not-so-old woman with flowing white hair. Her eyes were his eyes, slate blue, recessed, haunted. He paid and headed for the bus but turned back to search for her in the parking lot. Did he know her? She had vanished. Was the curtain mutating again, conning his senses with more sophistication? He had to stop this, stop seeing things that weren't there.

He collected his knapsack from the bus and nodded to the bus driver, whose relaxed face issued pleasure at recent urination. Lucky SOB, Stefan thought, You just don't know. The bus doors swished shut behind him. His bladder felt like a football shoved up his ass. Why him? He flushed and spat on the macadam. Damn stupid question; he was alive after all. Why him? He headed on foot across Route 37 past the bungalows on West End Ave. to see if the river had disappeared, too.

Stefan stood on the boardwalk and sipped his coffee. Its steam twisted away on river breeze. He watched a motorcyclist play, cut the corner too close at the open-air Pavilion, skid on the gravel where the Edgewater Hotel used to be, right the bike, and gun up the hill toward the delicatessen with the sustained racket of an M16's 90-round burst. Out of sight, the motorcycle backfired. Stefan dove behind a bench. The impact punched urine from his distended bladder.

He came to. Hanging off a bulkhead. Wet with sweat. Sprawled on a boardwalk. The scent of saltwater-logged hardwood signaled home. A few feet from his face, brown waves rocked and cradled a coffee cup. As he stretched to fish it out, the green plastic bottle of Excedrin fell from his shirt pocket and floated. Staring at the bottle as it bobbed on his reflection, he wondered if he was actually the reflection looking up at a bottle that half-hid his doppelgänger and the heavens beyond. Maybe he should hit the bottle. Maybe he already had. He sat up and patted his pockets for a flask. Finding none, he eyed his coffee-splotched shirt and yellowed crotch. The future smelled of piss.

He scouted the boardwalk for witnesses. At the far end of the bulkhead, an old man scooped a crab net from the water, inspected it, turned the net inside out, and shook back his catch. Must be less than 4½ inches, not a "keeper," Stefan thought. By law, the young crab was the river's charge. To check the waterfront panorama, he leaned back and right at the waist to compensate for his neck's downward tilt. Not a soul in sight except for the old man—just colorful Victorians on the rise facing the river and the expanse of blue sky between their gables and tall evergreens on the southern bank.

He stared again at his soiled clothing and knew that his mom, whose senses compensated for her deafness, would smell the urine even if he clenched his thighs. Aunt Syd would smell it, too, if she stopped off for lunch from her UPS job. What time was it? He upended the knapsack on his lap. No watch; he must have left it somewhere. After scouting again for spies, he hunkered down behind the bench and changed into a navy blue T-shirt and frayed cut-off jeans, commando-style, with the can of H_2Ocean shoved in a pocket.

His deaf ear's ringing fell silent. In its silence, peace amplified the lapping of river waves. The wind shifted, and spray over the bulkhead felt good and right on his desert-parched skin. He closed his eyes. The rhythmic lapping soothed, reached his desiccated senses. He gulped the salt-water air, the smell of wet rope, a full-to-bursting lungful of air that resurrected a feeling of something he once knew. He squeezed the crystal in his sore left ear so hard his eyes flew open, pinched, and teared. He yanked up the knap-sack flap, crammed in his sandals and soiled wet clothes, and leapt off the boardwalk onto sand—wet Jersey shore sand—and tore along the narrow beach toward his mom, Aunt Syd, and Moose while he sang a capella with the gulls, *I am coming home.*

The strong odors of fuel at the boatyard turned his stomach, but he didn't break stride, the familiar smell urging him on to the cove and the sun-dappled path that curved up-hill through firs to a clearing, his back yard, home. Just shy of the path, he keeled over except for his right foot, which stuck flat on the sand. He instantly knew, of course, what had happened, what is bound to happen when running barefoot anywhere near a boatyard. The nail in his heel attached to a plank buried in the sand. With piercing pain, he unearthed the board and thrust his full weight on it with his left foot. The nail released him.

His blood seeped into the sand. Just like the blood seeps into the sand despite the steady pressure of Stefan's hands on Juan's gaping chest. Juan, crack-up comic who's good for morale when the men slump into glum and grim. Juan, whose blood spews like geysers through Stefan's fingers. The whole convoy is under attack, and the medic is too many trucks back. Juan gurgles the word "keelhaul" until he dies, which makes no sense. Is he saying "kill all"? "Kahlil?" Stefan's deaf ear resumed its ringing.

Mind over body. Mind over brain. He sat on the damp sand and propped the wounded heel on his left thigh. In his pocket, the can of H_2Ocean, the healing saltwater spray, jabbed his groin, and urine spurted and stopped. Stefan set the can on the sand and rummaged in the knapsack for the coffee-stained shirt, which he tied tight around his foot. Pausing, as though responding to a muezzin's call from a mosque minaret, he prayed the prayer of watching helplessly as Juan died again on the back of his eyelids. Before he could think "Amen," a burning bush howled "*three* of ours," a smoldering beard yowled "three of *ours,*" and the breath of spring tide whispered "six of mine." The can of H_2Ocean toppled and rolled into the waves.

Hobbling, Stefan dragged the sodden plank to the scrub. He pressed the side with protruding nails into the sandy soil. No one else would get hurt now, not even a dog. He limped to the river, where small saltwater waves chilled the soles of his feet and stung the new wound. He waded in up to his calves, grabbed the floating can, and tossed it to the sand.

The river was shallow here, and he sat clumsily without leaning on his pierced heel. He lowered himself backward into the cold that shrank his testicles to walnuts. Rocked by waves, he half-floated, half-scraped the pebbly cove bottom. Above the saltwater scent, the fragrance of white pine and purple iris wafted down from his yard. It was May, almost June; the iris scent told him so. He sank his head into the cold. His right ear pulsed with the river's underwater roar, and his left ear sensed only a hum of pressure—the same song but heard in decibel extremes. One river yet an alpha and omega in his head. "F'ing A," Juan says with his contagious grin. "Amazin' O," Denzel croons in his laid-back drawl. Carl says nothing; he has no head.

Stefan came up for air and studied a quadrant of sky and tops of Loblolly and Eastern pines inland, from which gulls flapped to soar on the prowl over the cove. He shivered and shimmied out to deeper water, losing his makeshift bandage in the process, and swam, sputtered, and choked. The crawl, his favorite stroke, no longer worked; his fused neck held his nose under water. He switched to a backstroke and swam out past the cove so he could see downriver to the bay and the bridge beyond.

Noise exploded all around him. He searched the sky for incoming—nothing. He twisted in the water and spotted a motorboat upriver, its roar echoing off the banks as it bore down on the bay bridge and him in between. The water warmed between his thighs as his bladder released at last, and he waffled between physical relief and remorse—better to piss in a river than on a bus seat, but pissing in this river felt like blasphemy. Still pissing, he swam awkwardly toward the nearest land: the Point, his favorite beach, now deserted and abandoned to dune grass years ago.

As the motorboat passed, he hit the Point's sandbar hard and scraped the back of his neck raw. He limped ashore and sank dripping on the weathered bulkhead. River and bay gusts collided at the Point, and wind-whipped sand stung his neck. Shivering, he stripped off his wet shirt and rubbed his arms briskly. Across the expanse of river opening into Barnegat Bay, a Ferris wheel towered over a horizon of houses. For a moment, as he warmed in the sun, all felt right with the world. A fleeting thought. Naïve. But he added to his mantras: Blood is thicker than piss.

Heading back by foot, he stepped gingerly, heel to toe, pain every other step, and ringed the crescent of cove with bloodied footprints, which melted into themselves and ever-changing shoreline. Headed toward the path that led up to his yard above the beach to a mom whose face he could only half-remember. What would half her expression look like when she saw him limping in; saw his crooked, bleeding neck; when he couldn't show her a Purple Heart yet; when he confessed he could piss himself at any moment; when the thought first occurred to her that he'd lost his mind? He cringed at the thought of horror in her eyes. No curtain clouded *her* vision.

Damn the curtain. To protect his family from it, from him, meant heading to the depot for a bus bound to God-only-knows. To have come this far, this near, for nothing? "Mind over brain" didn't seem to be working. A rogue wave, precursor to high tide, licked his ankles. His toes burrowed in the sinking sand.

No choice. Leave. As he stooped to grab his knapsack, ancient sounds prickled his skin, his nostril hair. He jolted upright to face his good ear toward the trees, the hilltop, where barrel-chested Moose barked her recognition. Stefan felt sound then in his sternum, which thrummed with pitches of impatient yelping, of the whine and slam of a rusty-hinged screen door, of his mom who rarely spoke—never could pronounce his name—calling "TEFFA? *TEFFA!*", and of twig-snapping, leaf-crackling, heart-tackling love, still obscured by trees, spilling down the hill to greet him. Watching the boughs at the foot of the path, Stefan backed into the river and waited, crouching, braced for the leap of his dog and the unconditional whole of his mother's face.

The "Sandie Five"

The sandstone Shoprite in West Orange, New Jersey, towers tall yet hidden behind the hill graced by Macy's, Dress Barn, and Panera Bread in the Essex Green strip mall along Prospect Avenue. Hundreds of customers are flocking to Shoprite for emergency and impulse food shopping this Saturday, October 27, 2012. Normally dedicated to her budget and diet, Leah Croft, on Aisle 2, Coffee and Tea, hefts a heavy cylinder of 4C Iced Green Tea mix into her cart and crosses it off the list, at the bottom of which she has penned "Bad ☺" to mean some highly caloric delicacy, not yet decided upon, that will console her in the impending ninety-mile-per-hour winds. She unbuttons another notch, feeling a "private summer" hot flash and her claustrophobia kicking in as she's elbowed by all manner of folks preparing for Hurricane Sandy and PSE&G's

frightening first-ever announcement to expect power outages. Fear of the unknown starts to draw her down once again into a vortex of terror, but she resists out of habit, distracts herself with contemplation of what sweet delicacy she shall indulge in, but decides to postpone the decision, like a carrot on a stick, until she has purchased all the canned goods she does not want to eat.

"What is unisex?" asks a cute curly blond tot of her father, who wears an olive khaki-colored mechanic's uniform with "Steve" embroidered in Rutger's "Scarlet Knights" red on the chest pocket placket.

"You know what unisex is, sweetie," he says, glancing over at Leah and winking, "it's the church's little cardboard box you've been putting coins into for kids on World Sunday tomorrow."

"I hope your daughter's Sunday school teacher is as quick-witted as you, Steve." Leah winks back.

"Yeah, that Unicef conversation should be rich. I'm sure I'll hear about it. Happy shopping!"

"Thanks—you, too," says Leah, who moves on to Aisle 4, Canned Fish, etc., where she helps herself to several tins each of mackerel, sardines, anchovies, and mussels. She must remember to look for fresh-cut vinegary horseradish, since the creamy mild sauce in the refrigerator will turn bad once the electricity goes off. What aisle would fresh horseradish be on? Must be Fresh Produce. She skipped that aisle, where more people than she expected were helping themselves to greens. Those silver-haired yuppies in V-neck cashmere sweaters and pony-tailed joggers in Nikes and leggings must live on the mayor's street, which no doubt would retain electricity. Or maybe they can afford back-up generators.

Leah turns to pluck some canned corned beef hash from the opposite shelving and smacks into a middle-aged, green-bag-wielding female shopper dressed in a navy suit, all business on a Saturday and no humor in sight. Leah apologizes, waits for the discontented woman to pass, and picks two cans of the store-brand hash.

"And then you almost took the ramp toward Bayonne," says a lovely green-eyed redhead to Steve, who has appeared in Canned Fish now, too. "You knew we were headed for Newark Airport and Scotland."

Leah perks up and eavesdrops. Her significant other lives in Scotland.

"Bayonne? Scotland? They're pretty much the same," says Steve, straight-faced.

"Yeah," the redhead says, "lots of angry fat men wearing no pants."

Steve laughs so hard he drops a can of Hormel Chili on his hard-booted foot. "Hey, now, let's be politically correct."

"Actually, I am," she says with a self-righteous toss of her hair. She lifts their fidgeting blond toddler from the cart and sways her smoothly from side to side.

The chili can rolls to a stop at Leah's feet, and she returns it to Steve, who nods a smiling thank-you.

"Let's not forget *I'm* the one who ate the haggis, and *you* barfed on *me,*" Steve says to his green-eyed beauty.

"Watch it, I'll beat you with a stick," she threatens with mock fierceness.

"Promises, promises. Oh, look— 'Nessie Jerky,'" he says to his wife while pointing down the aisle.

"What? Where?" she asks.

With a Scottish burr, Steve says, "Loch your mouth on this jerky!" and he bumps his lower quarters into her belly, at which they smooch unashamedly and hold up hurried and harried shoppers behind their heaped carts.

When the couple moves down the aisle, gently touching at shoulders and hips, Leah feels lonely. She hasn't yet made a Skype account. Her Scottish boyfriend is clearly busy just now, yet his emails overflow with worry for her and his friends along the U.S. Eastern seaboard. She wishes he could be here to hold her snugly in his arms under the down quilt on her king-size bed when the house gets battered, although she admits with guilt that she should prefer him out of the hurricane's path.

Leah takes stock of her cart—all boring canned goods—and considers the "Bad ☺" on her list. There's only so much canned hash one can stomach. What shall she indulge in?

"Mop assistance required on Aisle 11." The voice on the public address system is too loud, perhaps to be heard over the hundreds of customers speaking over each other.

Aisle 7, Cookies and Baking Goods, is mobbed. Shoppers throng—no milling today—at the cookies end of the aisle. They, too, must be planning scrumptious off-diet respites, and baking will be out of the question. Within easy hearing distance, Leah observes a haggard, pasty-faced, bushy-haired young man in an oversized Army jacket. He is clutching in long white fingers a bag of ginger snaps, and his left eye quivers shut and open, shut and open, as he argues the wisdom of his spicy choice over the chocolate chip brand of his Hispanic girlfriend dressed in skin-tight red leggings and over-the-knee boots. What an unlikely pair they seem. They clearly can't decide on one brand of cookie but then exchange knowing smiles and happy shrugs, as if used to such an impasse, and toss both bags atop cartons of Pop Secret and Orville Redenbacher microwave popcorn in their cart. Maybe they live on the mayor's street, too, or are stocking up before driving west. Sensing their argument as a game they play, Leah envies their ease with and knowledge of each other. The odd pair embrace, and he entwines his white fingers in her glossy black hair, which brings to Leah's mind the sharp image of strange thin broken shells she found one year while beach-combing a cove along Toms River in Island Heights. Such decoratively pitted pure-white strands, no thicker than twine, and mixed in the sand with shiny obsidian shards, would create a gorgeous necklace if the jagged edges were polished smooth. When the Aisle 7 crowd disperses a bit, she wedges her cart in toward the cookies.

For some reason, the "Keebler" shortbread section has been hardly touched, shelves still brimming with colorful row upon row of yellow bags. Leah finds herself studying the leafy Hollow Tree logo and the white lettering of "Keebler" splashed across a red background. The colors make her think first of Valentine's Day and then the "bleeding snowman" in the Scottish courtyard last Christmas and the ketchup splotches on the snow-dusted cobblestones that she inadvertently tracked inside onto the wide pale planks of her boyfriend's kitchen floor, which she cleaned immediately and quietly along with her boot bottoms lest she trail the ketchup farther onto his Persian carpets and incur more condescending fault finding, an alarming and atypical pattern in his recent behavior. Maybe someone used to speak to him that way. If only he could remember that his angry tone stabs deeper than nails into people who suffer post-traumatic stress disorder. She hopes it's just a phase that passes before he breaches the final threshold of her PTSD, which will catapult her into full flight and self-preservation mode. Ironically, Leah thinks, maybe they are blessed to have a primarily long-distance relationship. But she loves him and wishes he were here; a healthy dose of his once-normal support and enthusiasm would be so very welcome right now. She selects two bags, one Pecan Sandies shortbread and one Toffee Sandies shortbread.

Leah loves shortbread and knows, as most cookie aficionados do, that the shortbread recipe dates back centuries to Arabian cuisine. She also knows what most people don't know: that Keebler was founded in 1853 in Philadelphia, Pennsylvania, where her Scottish immigrant great-great-grandfather used to work and gratefully accept over-baked "rejects," which his family, of course, never rejected. Pecan Sandies, a childhood favorite, always made her think of him with his silver hair and thin silver-rimmed eyeglasses, which enlarged watery Monet-like blue irises, per her grandmother's diary. If he were alive today—at age 179—he'd be up on a ladder at home stoically boarding up windows without a grumble, or more likely cursing up a super-storm.

With a flinch and a grin, it occurs to Leah why people might not be buying Keebler's Sandies. And yet how appropriate to munch on Sandies during Hurricane Sandy. Yes, Sandies will be her "Bad ☺" while she toughs it out. Talk about embracing your fear, she thinks, and imagines eating an entire bag's worth under the down quilt where she will huddle alone.

On Aisle 9, shelves are bare where the inexpensive bottled water would normally be. Leah finds an overpriced twenty-four pack, thinks about it, and resignedly adds another to her cart.

"It was like this yesterday, too," says a grimacing African-American man, who is trying to snare a plastic gallon of water with a prosthetic arm. A beer-bellied, unshaven fellow in a gray sweatshirt reaches over to assist.

Noting the humane gesture with appreciation, Leah still grinds her teeth as she crosses off "Water," the last item on her list. She can't stand wasting money. At least she has homeowner's insurance, so if the hurricane damages her house, she won't have to pay out of pocket. But she can't afford the time it would take to fix the house because her car lease is expiring soon, she can't get a home equity line due to "Insufficient Income," and she's way too close for comfort to the ludicrous situation of having to sell her house in order to buy a cheap used car—in which she'll have to live because she won't have a roof over her head anymore. Could Mother Nature have chosen a worse time for "the hurricane of the century," not to diminish Katrina's impact? How she hates this downward spiral, the sucking vortex that grips her in the economic recession and her own depression. That's two spiraling vortexes, Leah thinks, the hurricane and the economy. In her experience, spiraling vortexes usually come in threes. She wonders what the third one is. A marble-gray pigeon with pink-tinged wings flaps in front of her face and soars up to the rafters of the supermarket ceiling.

Leah checks herself for guano, finds none, and heads for the cashier lanes at the front of the store but is surprised by a new arrangement. Today, Shoprite has organized to queue customers in the dairy and bread aisle at the side of the store and wend along the back as necessary. A very official-acting young Asian manager with a dyed-blond buzz cut directs each customer to a lane once a purchase is finalized. Leah heads back down Aisle 9, can't get through the glut of carts and folks trying to buy water, and aims for the far corner via Aisle 11, where the spill has apparently been mopped up already. In the corner, at the end of the line, she stares at the milk there is no point in buying.

She tries to count the number of carts in front of her but can't see through all the taller folks. She imagines the orderly consumers awaiting their turns—alternately weary, hurting, bored, or cheery, each one leaning on his or her respective cart—a penitent queue approaching the pay-up confessional, a concept to which she, a Presbyterian, can bring no personal experience. She wonders if a Catholic can slip away with a clean and clear conscience on the deathbed. *Timor mortis conturbat me.* Blood on the lintel—futile in the wake of acts that are clearly not of God. The line moves up the length of the butter section, where Leah grasps a pound of Land o' Lakes Sweet Creamery Butter, admires the Native-American maiden on the box, thinks of baking and pressing cookies—peppermint Christmas trees, ginger camels, and cream cheese wreaths—and then puts the box back in its spot on the refrigerated shelf. When the power goes out at home, the butter will go bad long before the fresh Italian loaf, which she just now realizes she forgot to add to her list. "Give us this day our daily bread" takes on new meaning.

"Stop that, Timmy," whispers a woman behind her. Leah turns to see a happy mop-haired little boy, who is clearly too young to know the word for what he is doing. His eyes are rolling back in his head, and his legs are dangling out the front of the cart as he rises to full sitting height and lowers and rises, over and over, pressing his precious little privates against the firm wire mesh of the shopping cart. His motion simulates the carousel at Seaside Heights, where the horses sink and leap in grace and gilded garlands. Every year, she rides a mare named "Lillian," which is painted in green cursive on her flank. Lillian's pole is static, which Leah prefers to dizziness. The male creatures also stand fixed but line the outside edge of the circular floor, handsome and regal, especially Mike the camel, Walt the roaring tiger, and Leo the lion, whose curled lips and teeth are frozen mid-roar. At the center of the carousel hub, among sparkling mirror tiles that spin in and out of view, historical information is posted that she memorized in spurts maybe forty years ago: "Hand-carved Dentzel/Looff Carousel ... built circa 1910 ... real Wurlitzer ... military band organ." She wonders that she never photographed the carousel before. At least it's a snapshot long held in memory. She must remember to take her digital camera next summer.

It occurs to her then that she keeps fixating on her favorite places and not the here and now, the imminent threat, fear of the unknown to be thrust or not upon them all without prejudice in roughly twelve hours. And she must shoulder it alone. An audible sigh escapes her lips. Then, with fresh insight from somewhere, she perceives the huge supermarket as a microcosm of the global village and its citizens united in a common bond: surviving the upcoming unknown. They all have their own problems, and now this, the hurricane on top of it all. Parents put on brave and cheerful faces for their children. Some folks still believe "it" could never happen to them, no matter what "it" is. Believers. Nonbelievers. The worried. The afraid. The doom-sayers. The nay-sayers. The African-American woman with the blotched face and pain-riddled knees who wheezes and leans heavily on the push bar of her shopping cart. Leah knows how the woman feels. A short Slavic woman sports too-short bangs, which form a straight line between her limp hair and creased forehead; her shopping cart contains more cans of dog and cat food than "people" food. Leah figures she'll know how that feels soon, too. And then there are the truly admirable folks, maybe Catholics, maybe not, who simply live proactively and don't worry, wear optimism on their faces, and even make jokes, which makes the threat much more manageable for everyone else. She remembers reading in some psychology magazine that if you want to feel better, simply smile. She knows it works, and she smiles.

"Lane 12, ma'am," says the blond Asian manager, who in his black pants, starched and pressed white shirt, and tie, looks like a pilot but without the hat and a bar of wings.

"Thank you, sir," Leah says, still smiling.

As she unloads her canned goods and bottled water onto the conveyor belt, she suddenly realizes what the third spiraling vortex is—her own gullet—and she dashes back to Aisle 7, Cookies and Baking Goods, to scoop up a bag each of Simply Shortbread Sandies, Dark Chocolate Almond Sandies, and Cashews Sandies, bringing her Sandies stash to five. She smiles through the notion that she'll soon be sporting the "Sandie Five" like a "freshman fifteen"—desperate times call for mouth-watering pleasures—and feels perversely good about being so "Bad ☺".

Still smiling, she folds the cash register receipt into her wallet and checks the time on her cell phone. Not bad, only twenty-five minutes from the far corner to out the door, which under normal circumstances would probably cause her to seethe but today is impressive thanks to Shoprite's emergency organization. She rearranges the cookies in one of her Shoprite green bags lest they topple out.

"Ah, a Sandies lass," says a male voice beside her.

She turns in wonder and sees it's not her Scottish gent but rather an attractive, well-groomed man with, of all things, silver hair and silver-rimmed glasses.

"Ah, you found me out," Leah blurts.

"Care to sit out the storm with me? I've got a front-row seat on First Mountain," he says, with a glimmer of nothing but innocence on his face.

Leah can't tell whether he's a phenomenally good player, a jokester, or a sweet lonely widower seeking her company and chit-chat.

"No, but thank you," Leah says, "you just made my day. See you here next Saturday?"

"God willing. I'll bring popcorn and Sandies." And with that, he salutes her and is on his way, no doubt to First Mountain. Must be a lovely view.

It occurs to her that her smile was forced before but now feels radiant. Following the global villagers out the automatic door, she pushes her Sandies-filled cart into a deceptively balmy afternoon and the ubiquitous unknown, alone, but not.

Cleavage

Five minutes late for Geoff's reading at Fowey River U., you stride your black suede heels into Lostwithiel Library past the chevron-bricked lobby to the sunny Arbor Room, where you spot him up front, chatting with three admiring young female students. His hair glints more silver than a year ago. He's rolled up the sleeves of his black shirt with teal pinstripes in a rugged, sexy way. You do not love him.

Unable to manage eye contact yet, you thank the gods that his back is to you. But his back is to you, which sends up a red flag; he usually faces the door to gauge the scene. Your cheeks flame scarlet at the thought of his for-fun-only flirtatious emails and your liquor-soaked responses—keystrokes with no sense of propriety: "Let me drink from you; be my sustenance." Your clothes and dignity turn to glass. If he turns, his baby blues will see you nude.

You hide in the back row, and your sexy black pencil skirt rides too short up your thighs. You cross your legs and shift your bottom. Better—although a blue-haired lady in polyester stares up your muscled calves to your fitted silk blouse to your feathered hair, meets your eyes, looks away.

During the eloquent introduction, which you know by heart, your eyes drift from the faux marble tile floor to soundproofing tiles in the ceiling—twelve across by twenty deep—to young potted yews casting shadows on a mural of firs. Strange—no dust motes in this late afternoon sun. Geoff strides on applause to the podium. You center yourself on the back of a broad navy blazer, study the frayed end of a scarf casually slung over the shoulder. Geoff's voice, quavering—a first—washes through the room. You send him lapis blue light to calm his nerves. Clutched on your lap is his book, which you've read twice already. You float, cradled, on the rhythmic waves of his words.

Until— He can*not* be reading the scene about the conference five years ago. Your torso twitches. From twenty feet away, he reaches right through that massive woman you're hiding behind and pokes you square in the chest. Reaches through time itself to that very conference, when you won a raffle to meet with a famous author. A singular conference during which, on the penultimate day, you sat, hands in your lap, at the corner of a long antique mahogany table in a room with books shelved from floor to ceiling. The hypnotizing aromas of old paper, the glue in case bindings, Geoff's wool overcoat, his nasty chest cold. His hands paging through your short story manuscript, his right index finger pausing here and there, touching your words. As you listened to his mesmerizing voice, his kind comments and astute proposed changes, something unworldly, psychic, possessed you, forced you to feel an invisible cord binding your sternum to his, which ruffled your senses, flustered your passions. Observing your sudden fidgeting, he finished quickly, asked if you had questions. You said no, thanked him, and fled. Pondered the strange feeling for days. Wondered if you were lovers in a previous life. Dismissed it entirely as a strange symptom of jet lag or an eruption from the Muse of creative joie de vivre. Joined a master's program, were astonished to find him on the faculty there. As if it were all meant to be. But what all, what be? All too silly for credibility, you think. And yet—

"... synchronicity." Geoff's voice lingers on the word to signal the end of the passage, which is clearly the end of the passage, but he is an experienced reader and empathizes with his audience, with humanity. Applause ends your reverie.

As you join the long, languid flow toward his thick black autograph, someone behind you shrieks "Mekka!" It's Dona, a former classmate, a petite poet with jet-black hair in a stylish wedge, whom you haven't seen since you both graduated last year, the oldest two in a class of intergenerational students.

"Look at you!" Dona says.

"There are fringe benefits to divorce," you respond, stooping to hug her, remembering with pleasure her earth-mother embrace.

"I'm sorry," she says.

"I'm not," you say.

"Which explains your relieved and happy glow," Dona says. Her smiling eyes roam your face, pleased for you.

With lowered voice, you tell her that last year was a year from hell, the year you divorced your lying husband and suffered anorexia (forty pound's worth), inordinate fear, night after month of little sleep, and the suicidal rock bottom of the Betrayal Trench, a regular Bermuda Triangle where you longed for oblivion. Instead, into that maelstrom of agita and angst, up popped Geoff's email in your lonely inbox. You don't tell Dona about him but wish that you could. That he lived too far away, Vancouver, for in-person get-togethers, but he drank merlot and chatted online with you throughout the day, many nights, and you found self-preservation and the courage to rise, exercise, lift weights, three pounds to five pounds to eight, dream of springtime and sex. He was a good and kind friend to hold your hand figuratively through the typhoon of emotions, which he was weathering himself, still devastated by his partner-split. You held his hand in return, and he somehow surged into your heart like "you've got male" with a flood of libido in your nether regions—hardly part of any rational plan, but your heart and hormones didn't ask your brain first.

The autograph line moves up. You greet the man joining Dona, the always-smiling poetry professor, his beard and tweed jacket of complementary silvers and grays. A student interrupts, and you can't focus on his multi-syllabics over snippets of Dona's conversation now behind you: "never seen such a transformation … looks like Marilyn Monroe." Gross hyperbole, but you smile and stand straighter, gut and butt tucked in—shades of Miss Georgianna's charm class way back in sixth grade.

"Should I address this to you or someone else?" Geoff asks, not smiling, reaching for his book in your hands.

Too late to run. You swallow your tongue and point to your chest, are not sure then if he recognizes your more-svelte self. He's flushed as he writes "To Mekka" with great flourish. Is he ill? Your eyes trace the familiar G as he signs: Geoffrey. Not his customary autograph. Formal, far away. Your left breast grazes his right triceps. You jump back, regain proper territorial distance. As distant in time as Chaucer, for whom Geoff's parents had named him.

"Did you miss the reading?" he asks, still not smiling. Which is when you suspect that you screwed up—maybe he wanted, needed, to see you, greet you, *before* he read. Or maybe you've spun an intricate web of self-lies that trick your mind into playing masochistic games. Your explanation of rush-hour traffic sinks into mumble, and you step aside. So that's that. Dream dreamt. Reality sucks. What could you have been thinking?

Outside in oddly warm March air, you fish for your car keys, too confused to cry.

"Mekka." It's Dona, rushing after her. "The department will go out after the book signing—want to come?"

Back inside—you resist looking at Geoff—Dona updates you on her chapbook prep, then segues into the phenomenon of conversing with lesbians about the beauty of women, which is not a discussion, she says, men can have with men. You venture it's sociocultural and don't ask if she's suddenly switched sides of the fence. Then she's on to other tip-of-the-iceberg comments until Geoff and stragglers meander toward the door. Geoff doesn't look at you.

Outside in front of the gang, he says, "Mekka, I like your blouse." You could have intrigued with the name of its color, Aegean Sea Blue, been glib and gay, but no, your eyes drop involuntarily as you whisper thanks and blush. You look up to see Geoff crimson but beaming. Too big a smile? Is he laughing at your awkwardness? He wouldn't do such a thing—would he? Would you? Has anyone noticed your adolescent exchange?

At Rendezvous, a restaurant/bar in a converted railway station, complete with three-ton chandelier and stained-glass windows, you set your purse on a stool at Geoff's high table, chat with his friend, the smiling bearded professor, and drink a vodka on the rocks like it's iced tea in August because Geoff, king of the mixed message, once again won't look at you. You float to another table and, with Dona, stroke current students suffering lack of confidence. Share their fried calamari and memories of summer residencies in Rome. Promise to attend their graduation. Write their names on a napkin because you won't remember. Back at Geoff's table, you order another vod. It tastes weaker than the first, so you drink it fast, too. You can't look at Geoff. You watch the piano player, who checks you out to and from the restroom. Nice, to be acknowledged, sometimes even like that.

"Mekka."

Your questioning eyes, swimming in molecules of music pooled and reflected on the glossy black piano, catch up with your turning head, and you are looking into Geoff, who is looking into you and smiling in shadow. Who turned out the light over the table? Where did everyone go? He smiles so big, his eyes squeeze closed. You smile back in kind. Two people smiling at each other, blind. You ease up on your smile so you can see. So has he. He raises his glass to toast. You have only ice in your glass. Does a toast count if there's nothing to drink? You clink glasses in silence. You try to drink melt from the bottom of your glass. There is none. Your mouth says, "I tried," your shoulders shrug, and your head turns back to the piano. You tried. Tried to what? Tried to let your sabotaging other-self scare him away? You're so shit-faced—on only two Smirnoffs—that you're lost between psychological observer and participant, between twit and "intelligent person with advanced degree." What, now you're schizo? You're too old for this crap.

The light returns. You help the smiling, bearded professor count the gang's collected currency, which is cracked because you're crocked and he's been drinking Perrier. People rise. Stool legs scrape.

Geoff opens his arms for a hug and says, motioning to your blouse, "To a silk day. It is silk, isn't it?" WTF? Your brain can't form the words that your mouth can't produce. His smile crinkles his eyes shut again. Good thing—you'll lose yourself in them this close. You lean in to hug, barely touch, no mixed message there. You can't look back—a year must pass before you'll see him next—and you manage not to tumble down the steps when your right heel slips. The car drives itself home—guardian angels at work. You won't test them like that again. You try to look ahead, but the future yawns with boredom.

Four days later, he emails from Paris. You look fantastic, he writes. You perk up, but you won't hear from him for three weeks now while he's on tour in Europe, a different city or country every day or so. You brace for Geoff withdrawal. Plan A: Set your sights on the year-long horizon and roll with the waves, one day at a time. Plan B: Don't ever email him again; it's just an infatuation, or infantile desire, and it's over—or should be. Plan C: Try navigating the "land-ho," lounge-lizard route. Plan D: You're not a whore, so scratch Plan C and instead seek a shrink, one who's expert on hypomania, transference, and rebound relationships. Plan E: Scratch Plan D, and instead Google postmenopausal testosterone + intense sexual desire. Which it turns out is rare, but you've got it, per the blood test, but only for Geoff, who's older than you, so you're not a cougar, but that's no consolation.

The best is yet to come, Geoff always says. To pass time between work, the gym, you drink absinthe at home, surf BsideU.com, and study self-help manuals, which define infatuation as three months long. Odd—you've been infatuated with Geoff for a year. Actually three considering you were probably in denial the first two. Why do the emails feel so real, the fleeting moments of real him, in person, a dream shimmering in mist? Is it the L word wrapped up in Möbius-loop bows of illusion, or delusion? You shiver, sip more absinthe, recall his flushed smile, wear it like dew. Wear it like the mirrored last image adrift in his eyes: fitted blouse—silk—Aegean Sea blue. Patient blue. True blue. More like hungry-loins you or "fifty-five going on sixteen" you. This is not normal. You weren't always shallow, not to diminish Geoff's virtues. Have you always been hormonally challenged? No. So how can you teach your heart that desire isn't love? Is it even possible now—old dogs, new tricks, and such? Back to square one.

With legs up on the sofa, new dog at your feet, and Augustine Pinot Noir in a crystal goblet this season, you're still exchanging emails but less frequently and with no hint of flirtation. Your emotions have calmed. Stable is nice. And then he sends a summer photo, you can't take your eyes off his bulging biceps, and you send a photo back, a low-cut tank with skirtini, which you always wear around the house. He messages three times, commenting on your "worthy cleavage." And up pops your libido—creaming your panties like you're a teenager again every time his name pops up bold in your inbox.

The Pinot Noir is smooth, no tannins. You pour another glass. You reflect on the relationship, how the titillating highs of your roller-coaster emotions give you vertigo, how his mood swings send you around the bend, how your mood swings can plummet him to the depths of rage—all via email. You decide, calmly and maturely, that someone must cancel this amusement-park ride: either care for him enough to spare him you, or care for yourself enough to spare you him. No other options sail into view, other than keep loving this man however he wishes, so you choose to sleep on it but second-guess yourself and suspect procrastination. Then you third-guess yourself and wonder if he, perhaps infatuated with you but still shy, is thinking the same thing.

"Mekka," you chide yourself, "you're fifty-six—time to grow up."

You raise your goblet toward Vancouver, toast this mesmerizing man who's been lighting your world, and bid a silent and caring adieu to what surely must be lunacy. You take another sip, drain the goblet, and cry until tears drip off your chin, tickle down your cleavage, your sternum. Which is when you start laughing. Sure, adieu, for six hours until you change your mind again—could be six minutes this time. Or six seconds even, which, in fact, is how long it takes you to start daydreaming about seeing him in March at Fowey River U., when you will probably again wear that fitted silk blouse, Aegean Sea blue, with an extra button, maybe two, undone. What's wrong, really, with a little cleavage between friends?

PART TWO

Valleys and Peaks

White Chin Hair and the Lonely Female Cardinal

You wake with a start. The clock's red LED numbers on the top shelf of the light-hued Scandinavian computer hutch in the corner say 8:32, and you're surprised the morning birdsong hasn't awakened you sooner. Not really—you sleep later and later these days. You peek out the shade. No car in the driveway. Your daughter must have left early for church. Nature calls immediately, as it always does now, and the TV and high, neatly-arranged DVD stacks on the bureau obscure the reflection in the mirror of everything below your nude upper torso as you rush past and bounce only once off the doorframe—once being a nice change.

During ablutions, while you critically assess your physical self in the mirror above the sink, you recall the titillating words of a sweet silver-haired man who looked up at you mid-"dalliance" a week or month ago. "You have the breasts of a teenager," he had said with boyish glee, his face aglow. Which now makes you toss your once-brunette, then-white, now-platinum-blond mane in a happy perky shy way that ill suits your new age of sixty but not your current state of mind. Your divorce from that expletive-deleted deserter will be final soon, and it seems important to take stock of things anew. One thing at a time, you've learned, one compartmentalized area of your brain at a time—otherwise, the whole picture looms panoramic and overwhelming as a tidal wave. The bathroom mirror doesn't reveal the whole picture. Since this seems to be the day you will take stock of your physicality—and why not, church doesn't do it for you anymore, and your unemployed days for months have been spent in little more than stupor—you sashay naked down the hall to your daughter's room and the full-length mirror on her closet door.

The light is brighter here. The crooked scar radiating out from your right nipple, where a suspicious mass one-quarter the size of your breast was excised from the inside, is fading with time. (You don't remember the pain.) Post-biopsy, the mass proved to consist of not one but five precancerous tissues. For two years post-surgery, the nipple remained numb, which creeped you out sufficiently that you simply stopped touching it, and your husband, still around then, had long before lost interest in your nipples—and your mind, for that matter.

At least the surgeon sewed you back up so that it still looks like a breast. Most of the women on both sides of your family had their breasts lopped off during their fifties but too late to save their lives. Grateful to be alive and still have your right breast, you cup it and touch the nipple, feel the nipple feel the touch, watch the nipple perk up hard, feel the pleasant sensation lower down. Which makes you laugh—you'd assumed since youth, even though no one ever told you, that sexual desire just stopped, like growth of wisdom teeth and menstruation. Seriously, what mother would speak of such a thing? Would you tell your daughter? Maybe. When she's forty or fifty. Whenever she realizes life is not a never-ending promise.

A promise of what, you wonder. That seems an issue for another day, and you glance at your inner arms and sigh. You've been heaving those eight-pound dumbbells backward over each shoulder for months now, and you've still got wrinkly jello to show for your dedication. Despite the forty pounds you lost, sick with betrayal and hypomania, after your husband left. You don't want to marry again, so what difference does it make what shape your body is in, you wonder. Tons, you answer. You care, you're right to care, and that's what counts—taking good care of yourself, jello and all.

Your eyes scan lower, down to the waist that was always too wide. A twelve-inch difference between bust size and waist and between hip size and waist? Only a man could have determined those dimensions, which you tried futilely to fulfill for far too long. Was any female ever 36-24-36? Maybe Marilyn Monroe, but look what it got *her*. Or Barbie. No, actually she's about 5-3-5 and if proportionately human size would lack the requisite body fat to menstruate—no biological babies for Barbie. So you're stuck with 39-33-37, which isn't really that displeasing, you decide. Except when you look at that wrinkled pouch (as wide as your hip circumference, and why can't the proverbial "they" cut clothing for this particular problem) that juts out above the six-inch-wide Caesarian section scar, where another surgeon's knife (you don't remember the pain) bisected a muscle, which now can't fulfill its original design. But the scar, you conclude, performs a most beneficial function; it mirrors the smile on your face every time you think of your daughter, and what greater joy is there than that.

Moving on, your eyes settle on the saddle bags, which for whatever reason you never worried about. Down to the knobby knees. The right knee bulges more than the left, permanently swollen, where yet another surgeon's knife (you don't remember the pain) performed an arthroscopy when you were fifty to trim both jaggedly torn lateral and medial menisci and to remove the shredded ACL. A surgery usually performed on professional football players who are bashed, thrown, and then buried below a massive heap of Hulk-size men. All you did was step on your dog's leash, as the obedience trainer instructed, your dog bolted, the bottom half of your leg turned one way and the upper half the other. Your next conscious thought registered the "huh?" of parking lot gravel poking you in the back as you looked up at sky. No matter that you couldn't walk for three weeks or that the recovery period lasted fourteen months, not three. Water under the bridge. You've mastered the exercises that keep your quads strong enough to compensate for that mysterious ACL, which looks like a thin stick of gum but is deceptive, has incredible tensile strength, weaves through the knee and maintains its stability under normal, but not all, circumstances. You bow and give quads their due.

Your calves, nicely curved and muscled, pass muster. Your feet are too tiny for your height, which is why you're a klutz and can stumble on a wisp of dandelion fuzz, but men seem to like tiny feet. Especially with toenail polish. Why should it matter, your feminist self demands. Because you care, you answer. Because you want a man again. As absurd as that may seem at age sixty. Or maybe it's not absurd. No one ever told you about that either.

So your body "is what it is"—damn the cliché—and can only get worse, not better. Yet that's OK, you decide with maturity. Which is when you gasp and spin terrified to face your daughter's bed. No one is there. Not like a few Sundays ago when you thought you had the house to yourself so didn't bother to shut your bedroom door when you catered to your personal "whims," indulging in sighs and moans fit for a celebratory queen, only to discover with horror once your daughter returned from church that her boyfriend was lying upstairs in her bed the whole time—and wide awake, he made a point of telling you later, but with no telltale smirk or horror of his own. Not the sort of embarrassment you ever expect at age sixty. Falling and breaking a hip, sprouting a dowager's hump, yes, but not ... you can't even give this unspeakable thing a name. You shudder. Hardly auspicious for the decade to come. Your shoulders hunch.

Car tires crunch gravel in the driveway. You race into your room to dress. Black jeans, a V-neck teal sweater. You take the stairs quickly, hand gripping the rail tightly—second nature for ten years now since the knee fiasco—anxious to bask in the joy on your daughter's face after she teaches Sunday school. Where is she? You open the back door, which she forgot to lock on her way out, again. No car in the driveway. You hear the faint strains of "Neverland"—your hearing's still keen—and race back up the stairs for your cell phone in your pocketbook, tucked under the bed in case of burglary (like burglars would fail to look there).

"Hey, Mum," your daughter greets you. "I forgot to stop at Panera. My treat. Do you want anything?"

"Are you driving while you're talking on the cell phone?" you ask.

"I'm at the red light at Eagle Rock and Mt. Pleasant." Her undisguised disgust lowers the pitch of her voice.

"Sorry, sweetie. It's that 'ole Mom thing'."

"Now the light's green. *What do you want?*"

"Lemon-poppy-seed-muffin-large-dark-roast-coffee-thanks-hon."

"No-prob-Mom-love-you-bye," your daughter mimics. Her "love-you" means she's already forgiven you, but she's off the wireless line before you can say "love you, too."

You wander back downstairs to the kitchen where you nuke a cup of Irish Breakfast tea before you realize how dumb a move that is, coffee and all on its way. On the sofa in the living room while you're sipping your tea—which you'll throw down the drain as soon as you hear tires on the driveway again in order to avoid the embarrassment of explaining how quickly you forgot *blah-blah-blah*—you hear a strange sound in the kitchen. Probably just the Rose of Sharon branches brushing the windows. But it repeats. *Flap-tap-whoosh.* Again. And again.

Your steps across the Berber carpet are silent, and you tiptoe barefoot on the vinyl flooring past the basement door to peer around the stove. A female cardinal perches in the Rose of Sharon. She flings herself full force into the window, *flap-tap,* falls in a *whoosh* to the outer ledge, and peeks up and inside to the little ceramic statue of three open-mouthed hungry chicks, not cardinals, on the inner sill. She retreats to the Rose of Sharon and repeats her dangerous, flinging *flap-tap-whoosh.*

You can't bear the thought of her breaking her neck. Before you can rap lightly on the window, she's gone in a flash of rustling leaves. A pair of cardinals, which mate for life, adopted your backyard years ago, and the joy of their presence dissolved over time into something you took for granted. You recall seeing the male, a handsome scarlet fellow, last Spring. It can't be empty-nest syndrome crazing the female; it's October. Has a neighborhood cat caught her mate? Has he died of old age? You wish you could help this suffering female before she commits suicide.

"Neverland" plays again.

"I'm stopping at Shoprite, too," your daughter says. "We're out of milk. Want some fresh salmon for dinner?"

You try to explain in a somewhat hysterical confused rush about the female cardinal, but your daughter's in a rush, too. "Mom, *what do you want?*"

You agree to salmon and find yourself standing at the kitchen window weeping. "What *do* you want?" you ask yourself. The tears run to your chin before you wipe them with your hand and feel the stubble of one thick, strong, stubborn fiber, which you somehow missed during the neck- and chin-shaving ritual that—so help you, you can't think of in any way other than masculine—is now part of your daily feminine ablutions. At the downstairs bathroom mirror, it seems the stubble is invisible. Well, not quite, you discover. It's still a miracle, though. Your chin hair is finally turning white—you won't have to shave anymore! At which you suspect you've wasted the morning on shame-on-you shallow ruminations.

Back at the kitchen window, you bend that stubborn sole stubble this way and that with your index finger as you ponder again what you want out of life between now and the promise of life's end. In your mind's eye, you see reflected in the kitchen window the flame of a lone candle. It is night, and the soft shush of snow outside turns the landscape into a pointillist painting, coats the ground with a warm, downy quilt, heaps high atop the bird-feeder for the lonely female cardinal (you feel her pain). In the window's reflection, you see yourself alone (you feel your pain). Then a man with a white beard joins you, hands you a glass cup of eggnog laced with rum. He rubs his beard against your cheek, your chin.

You rub back and smile, secure in the knowledge that he can't feel your white stubble against his, that he knows you have white stubble, that he doesn't care a whit about it. As the peace outside and in envelops you, his arm circles your not-24-inch waist, and you respond in kind. *That simple,* you think. It's hardly a young girl's dream. Is it the dream of the inner child in your sixty-year-old body? Maybe so. A winter-tale dream for comfort, or an "After" photo if you wish for more than dreams.

The driveway gravel crunches. You wake from your winter tale, wish for more than dreams, and smell the coffee, rich, mellow, and round.

The Threshold of Things Lost

Angie's bare left foot, finally warm, trailed in the tea-brown water of Toms River, which had borne the ocean's cold through Barnegat Bay and upriver. She grasped with studied care the weathered gray plank on which she sat, the wood deceptively smooth but full of splinters, as she'd discovered often before learning to beware. Evening tide was rising to her left, and tips of waves burped through a rotted hole in the bulkhead, pooled, and rippled over smooth white and gray pebbles in a sand sinkhole to her right. She dipped the big toe of her tanned right foot into the clear pool, and her foot tensed and jerked, toes white and curled under from the cold. Left foot warm in three feet of brown river; right foot cold in a puddle of clear river—same water; weird, she thought. Gusts of salt-water breeze teased the cilia in her nose and swept her purple bangs into her eyes. Facing the lowering sun, she sneezed.

On the porch, Deirdre was fighting to beat her own Hearts record—thirty-five straight wins—and crapped out on twenty-nine. Where was Angie this time? Too worried and pissed to pass time with FreeCell, Deirdre cast about for something else to do. She really should fine-tune her article, "Loving Your Teen," due Friday to a popular psychology magazine, but she moved the laptop to the side table with finality. At her feet, their fluffy American Eskimo puppy raised its head, expectant. Leaning her head back on the tall rocking chair, Deirdre scanned the panorama of and through the three walls of floor-to-ceiling screens. No Angie, no pink bike. Nobody in sight. She rocked and waited and feared and fumed.

The SUV driver faced upriver, the better to observe the purple-haired girl. Salty sweat, which soon stung his steel-gray eyes too much to ignore, ran from his stubby white crew-cut down behind the binoculars. He rubbed his eyes hard, blinked, rubbed them again, smoothed his scraggly wild eyebrows, and wiped the sweat onto navy twill pants, caked with dried dirt from baggy knees down to muddy Dockers boat shoes. He zoomed in on the girl's tan face with its glowing skin, perfect but for a zit on her chin, her innocent eyes and moving lips lost in what could only be a love song. Zoomed closer, down—slender, a blossoming child, so near the cusp of virginity lost.

The screen door whined and slammed behind her. Deirdre knelt painfully to plant the cheery orange Gerbera daisies in the garden bordering the walk and wraparound front porch. She shifted her weight to her right rump, legs askew behind, and reached for a pot. Her limbs recognized their position before her brain did. The memory surfaced and popped; her body was mimicking the lame young woman in Andrew Wyeth's *Christina's World.* She shifted her legs out of Christina's pose and pulled her hair back—into Christina's windswept ponytail bound at the neck.

The high wind on the river a block away swayed the tops of oaks but diffused past pines and summer homes into a gentle breeze that rustled leaves of the Andromeda bush between Deirdre and the porch steps. God knows how it thrived, their "miracle bush." It had sprouted from the low stump of a dead Eastern pine when she was Angie's age. What was the Andromeda myth? Something about a princess chained to a rock. She couldn't remember why just then because her body superheated. Hot-flash sweat dripped from hairline to chin and off, down to her leaf green T-shirt now dotting with wet. In the winter, she'd rush outside. In the summer, she'd flee inside to ceiling fans and air conditioning. She rocked hard for momentum to rise, butt in air, no grace at all, and limped up the steps through the screen door, all to fight with the door between porch and living room. The top half of the door framed glass, which couldn't be pushed without breaking the pane. The bottom half, wood swollen with humidity, demanded a hard shove, which shot pain through Deirdre's arthritic left hip. Damn door, damn hip, damn sweat. TV blare assaulted her ears, and AC spilled past, cooling the air quicker than her body. Damn Angie and her disappearing acts. Deirdre wished she could stop caring so much because the love just led to worry, then anger, even seconds of hate, and she hated hating or feeling angry with anyone, let alone her only daughter.

He zoomed in even closer with the binoculars, down to the gardenia henna tattoo above the teal tube top swaddling her small right breast, to the nub of her nipple, down to the khakis cut to booty-short length, so short their fringe must surely merge with stray strands of muff. A mink mound. Mount. Mother, may I, he asked, looking up and inward, hoping for permission before his crotch grew untoward and revealed his sin.

The wind picked up with the rising tide and swept strands of Angie's long purple hair into her playful eyes, which indoors looked brown but here in sunlight sparkled with peridot facets in a sea of moss green. The curled end of her ponytail, bound high on her crown, tickled the nape of her neck, which she rubbed as she studied the brown waves. From upriver, crests collided in a rhythmic *slap-smack* this side of the channel marker, a bobbing orange buoy fifty feet out in the river. Not the pounding crash of ocean surf, but a *slap-smack* like out-of-synch applause catching on from the shore along the stretch of sandbar, known here in town as the Point.

The blaring TV hurt Deirdre's ears, but her mother couldn't hear much over the noisy air conditioner, whose frosty air began to soothe Deirdre's skin. The news anchorman announced yet another beheading of a kidnapped hostage and another American soldier blown to dismembered shreds in Afghanistan. And what the hell for, thought

Deirdre. So their mothers can shrivel up like old corn husks, their freedom to love rammed down their throats by a plunger run amok? The hot flash waned, and she shivered. Where the hell was Angie this time? Deirdre made herself acknowledge that she wouldn't be angry if she didn't love Angie so much, and if she didn't love Angie so much, she wouldn't fear for her to this degree. Of course, Deirdre still felt warped by her own rape decades ago, and she hated the uncountable fears that resulted from that trauma, hated that no parents could ever completely protect their children, hated fearing that her fears for Angie could exploit her tortured imagination and grow into real, tangible nightmares, a self-fulfilling prophecy.

Mother, may I, please, he asked again, anxious now, a twill tent above his crotch. Begin, rasped the voice, so gravelly it conjured the image of a crone, complete with cast iron pot over sparking, spitting fire. Begin, my son. With his left hand holding the binoculars, his right reached to unzip, and he coaxed and rubbed and tugged as though his manhood could sprout to the cave of his open mouth. His buttocks tensed, and a spring in the seat whined with his violent motion.

The water, though shallow, was brown as strong tea, too dark to see much through. Below her left foot, shadows darted. Could be crabs hunting for a succulent toe snack. Angie lifted her foot from the river, watched the drips fall and ripple in the low waves and dapple the gray plank on which she stretched, felt the warm air cool on her wet skin.

Then she grabbed her sneakers and scanned the pebbly sand and grass as she hip-hopped around discarded crab pincers and holly leaves toward the lone picnic table on the secluded public lawn.

"Mom, have you seen Angie?" Deirdre called over the blaring anchorman to her mother, Lavinia, a gray-haired woman whose legs lay crossed on the recliner's footrest—legs streaked with the purple lightning of varicose veins. Wasted again, in more ways than one, Deirdre noted—the booze was now swallowed by a shrunken version of the image in memory from a year ago still dressed in pink shorts and piqué polo top. Lavinia didn't stir. "Mom! Have You Seen Angie?" Deirdre's anger with Angie shrank to make room for the old drunken shrew from whose womb she'd sprung, Mom, an image of decay and what Deirdre feared becoming.

Two-point penalty, pausing. He dropped the binoculars to the passenger seat and began anew. His power engorged. To spill thy seed is blasphemy—the shrew voice screeched, which clawed at his scabs, threatening new wounds. Gasping, he stopped and looked up at the purple-haired girl, who was distant unmagnified yet next now and soon.

At the picnic bench, Angie faced the sparkling bay but with peripheral vision saw sun glint off something amidst the trees. It was probably cellophane litter, but she pretended it was an admirer with a camera. She'd learned to entertain lenses two years ago, to play right to them yet tune out onlookers' eyes and focus on counts of Color Guard routines—thrilling saber, rifle, and flag tosses, pliés, sotés, and jazz runs through rows of marching band members. But such thoughts linked with her sweet Jono, so far away, and she forced herself to live in the moment, to concentrate on the thrill of cumulus clouds racing through blue sky to hover briefly between her and the sun until its beams broke through and warmed her world again.

Lavinia struggled to clear her throat in the familiar, drawn-out, drowning gurgle. Her eyes remained lost in her crossword puzzle, but she acknowledged Deirdre's question with one of her own. "Is she in her room?" She ignored the booming cable news channel. Over the years, she'd perfected her method by combining mental stimulation and sensory shutdown—the news worked; reruns of *Get Smart* did not. Now, oblivious to the noise, Lavinia could lose herself in the puzzle, rise to its challenge, master it, float above her species and the bed it had made, above the frustrated image of throwing her first baby and dislocating its hips, above the limp that Deirdre could have conquered if she'd truly tried, above the maternal instinct that now drove Deirdre's concern, beyond thinking the unthinkable, out to where she, Lavinia, controlled the world—a world where she and she alone glowed without guilt. She reached for the whiskey sour, shining amber, ochre, and sienna in facets of cut glass. The ice cubes tinkled, but the TV drowned them out.

Angie lifted her long, firm, acorn-tan legs under the picnic table and rested her heels on the opposite bench. Pressing her knees down to counts of thirty, she stretched her hamstrings to shape up for band camp, just two weeks away, then junior year and the All-States Championship at Giants Stadium. For the newspaper photographers, band parents, admirers, for the judges in the sky, she arched her spine, shoulders back, boobs out, flashed a confident smile, and exuded proper performance "-tude."

In the beginning, the hag's voice had preached, just like his mother, who in life had commanded his allegiance as a weakling husband always defers to a domineering wife, who in death still demanded his fear and meek subservience. He groaned as he climbed over the seat, bracing with his right elbow, still working his left hand and swelling into his power. With his right, he reached into the back cargo area for the loop of rope. His mind leapt ahead. In the tussle, strands of the girl's purple hair would mat, and he'd sweep them back along her head like an angel's wing. He raised his eyes to window level to spy on the girl, who thrust her chest out—right at him. He opened his mouth to tongue and suck her nipples, and his fluid surged. All things in MY time, the crone warned with dictatorial authority. Always obedient, he turned back to his mission.

Angie's third varsity letter, SATs, the prom, Jono with his shy smile, the protective feel of his big, gentle hand cupping her left shoulder. Jono, a head taller than she, always stood to her right, the better to see her with his good eye. Angie swore both his eyes, darkest brown like rich earth, could see inside her. In her backyard last year, she was helping him with his counts so he wouldn't collide with other band members on the field. The crackle of crisp, autumn leaves released a musty spice as they side-stepped through them with precision; their flexed left legs with pointed toes crossed in front of their right legs in fluid motion. The ripple and snap of her saffron silk flag, his awesome sax solo, their simultaneous "shiz"—their euphemism for "shit"—when she missed catching a quad, the rifle smashing through leaves and thumping butt-first into a pile of puppy poop, her "gak," his "gross," his deep rumble of laugh, the hunt for the pooper-scooper that ended in the garage, where dust motes swirled around his haloed head, his lips sought hers, and desire dampened her panties for the very first time.

Enter, the voice commanded. Afire with his violent foreplay, he yanked the pink-flowered panties in his mind to her knees and thrust himself in lest he spill his seed.

"She could have gone to the Bay Beach, but without a tag, I can't imagine the lifeguard would let her stay. Unless the lifeguard's a he, and he likes purple hair." Deirdre waited for a response. Stupid move that—there wouldn't be one—and when would she learn. Her mother's pinched lips and furrowed brow whenever her granddaughter entered the room spoke well enough her opinion of purple hair, tube tops, and a mother who would permit such "immorality"—a mother who, at Angie's age, rebelled passively and changed each morning into miniskirts stored in her locker at school. But what kind of a grandmother detests her granddaughter? Deirdre watched Lavinia swirl her third whiskey sour of the day, the cut glass reflecting the khaki light on the TV news screen. Watched her sip once, twice, and return the glass to the wet cork coaster.

This one would fight him, hard—all the better, all the more fun, his scrotum slamming between her thighs—but she would succumb like all the rest, flushed and slippery with sweat, to his power.

They'd practice again this fall, sweet Jono and she. But it was summer still, and Angie was passing time during the family's annual shore trip, glowing warm in memories, anticipation, and sun. "In your gaze, I lost my place," she half-hummed, half-sang, pining for Jono, who was off in Colorado at computer camp on some mountain where his cell phone wouldn't work.

Deirdre sighed, bemoaning her fate as daughter to a lush, and winced upstairs to the bedroom she shared with Angie. The mussed sheets of Angie's bed lay twisted but flat, not molded to svelte limbs of a sprawled teenager. Her husband's mid-nap, air-grasping snore exploded from the adjacent room and ricocheted down the hall. Why Clark refused to get tested for sleep apnea once loomed as enigma, but she'd given up trying to understand and given up worrying that he'd stop breathing in his sleep. Given up long ago, before the Mideast mess, before their arrangement of separate sleeping quarters, before his guarded footfalls woke her in the night when he left Angie's room. Did he think she wouldn't hear? Did Angie love him too much to tell, her awakening face so innocent and happy as she sang, hummed, each day into being. Could a mere child deceive so well? Or was it all nothing more than Deirdre's morbid imagination? Did Clark only watch with love as their daughter slept, just as Deirdre had watched over the crib, pondering in joyful wonder her reason for living? Of course that was it. She wished she weren't so suspicious, so paranoid. The TV announcer's words boomed through the floor just as Clark gasped for air and the old bedsprings squealed when he lurched awake and fell back heavy into sleep. It sounded like the announcer said "Amber Alert." Good God, not another.

The hag croaked the syllables like an ancient language: A-noin-teth. His seed exploded into the girl in his mind, not one drop spilt. No one could ever say he *broke the rules.*

Why couldn't Angie come home before worry wrecked the day? Was it really too much to ask? Deirdre's concern mushroomed into black clouds of anger, which she feared as much as her fear of her fears. Could her anger function as a beacon for evil, materializing itself into a physical body, committing travesties she'd never have been able to imagine if not for her rape those many years ago and the unexpected snippets of horror on TV that further poisoned her mind before she could flail for the remote?

His hands sagged. His eyes closed. His head nodded, and his forehead thudded into the metal door handle. The pen in his shirt pocket fell and rolled between the seats. This, the seventh day, he hungered to save another. He raised his eyes again to window level and the purple-haired girl at the lone picnic table and the curve of her thighs and the oh-so-narrow strip of fringed fabric at her crotch and the cave of anointing and the burst of his seed, no not yet, and the plan maybe puppies this time and the victory over flailing arms and legs you must make them angels in spite of themselves and the flimsy veil at her cave and the rip through protest and flesh and the rapture sucks his seed in surging ocean swells you are blessed and, no not yet, and the plan maybe candy this time suck me purple. Mother, may I again, he croaked. The girl's perfect teeth would ring his pride like pearls.

"In your gaze, I lost my place," Angie sang as she lost her place in the clouds, which stretched to mountains in Colorado and Jono and love.

Clark rolled over on the lumpy old mattress and sank again toward an elusive winged mermaid, ever out of reach, whose purple tail swished through wispy clouds, soared to stratosphere and stars.

👁

From the head of the stairs, Deirdre called down to Lavinia, "Where is the Amber Alert? Does the pedophile behead his victims?"

Lavinia's hazel eyes, diluted with age and the fluid hue of her whiskey sours, glanced up, startled, but then returned to the printed cells of her crossword page. "What Amber Alert?"

"Oh, for God's sake," Deirdre swore under her breath at the foot of the stairs. She limped to the remote on her mother's armrest and clicked the TV off. "I'm going out to look for her."

Lavinia grabbed the remote and clicked the TV back on. "Aha!" She penciled letters into her crossword puzzle with a girlish glee, incongruous with her bony, age-spotted years yet oddly in harmony with her prissy-pink piqué.

"Bye," Deirdre said.

"Um-hmm," her mother mumbled, baffled already by the D joining 3-ACROSS and 6-DOWN.

👁

He came in his mind, but his body still craved. Through the window, he ogled the old lady dressed in pink at the picnic table and her Hitlerian love and the lash of her forked tongue.

With the puppy as her shadow, Deirdre gathered her keys, glasses, and purse from the lace runner on the buffet. Glancing up at the mirror that spanned the wall, she did her usual double take—shock at the mirror's misportrayal. Her hair was white, still, and she'd forgotten to shave her brunette chin hairs this morning. Why did she feel thirty-five inside, an image visible only deep in the blue of her eyes, where her inner child was missing today. Gone AWOL with Angie? Gone forever? Reaching for her white linen jacket draped on a dining chair, she changed her mind and left it. Had to get away from sordid news, the image in the mirror, her drunken mother, snoring Clark. Had to find Angie. Had to restore her inner child. Was she running away or running to? Both? And does a single soul give a crap? Surely not Clark, who she'd vowed to stand by in sickness and in health, in poverty and pride, in lust and limpness—vows she sorely regretted, yet she'd do it all again for precious Angie.

He came in his mind, but his body still craved. Through the window, he craved culpable Clark, who flopped on the picnic table like a fish out of water and fluttered limp after purple tail.

Wanting no distractions, Deirdre left the puppy forlorn inside the back screen door. She backed out the driveway, past where the honeysuckle and sassafras used to grow, and mapped her circular itinerary: playground, gazebo, Bay Beach, library, marinas, Pavilion, deli, Point Beach, home. Not really home. The family shore house was a home away from home, but if ever given the option to click ruby heels, she would fly home to here, where peace always reigned, or used to anyway, back when she was thirty-five, pre-marriage, pre-child, when all seemed as it should be, the good old days, except for her mother.

He came in his mind, but his body still craved. Through the window, he craved angry Deirdre, who flailed at clouds of fear, worry, and hate that threatened to consume her, the picnic table, and all of Point Beach.

Deirdre minded the speed limit rather than test her guardian angel as she'd done on 9/11, when she topped 85 speeding down Garden State Parkway from work to Angie's school, too frantic to notice the clouds of dark smoke roiling and spewing on the eastern horizon. Today, though, she knew she was over-reacting in yet another manifestation of separation anxiety, which even Angie had mastered the first day of kindergarten. By contrast, Lavinia loved having the house to herself when the kids were in school, back in the *Leave It to Beaver* days, and she'd told them just that, often. How the hell did she think that made them feel, Deirdre wondered for the millionth time, and for the millionth time tossed the thought of that and 9/11 to the Garbage Bag of Crap in the back of her brain that leached down to her stomach and colon.

Neither Angie nor Jono told their parents of their dream: to provide humanitarian aid in the Mideast next summer. One person can make a difference, and two, so much more.

Anointeth my angels, my son, came the answer, her voice a whisper that ricocheted off crusted razors. He drooled in anticipation of foreplay and climax and all the wet, like at Massah and Meribah, the place of testing and quarreling, where Moses struck the rock at Horeb and water flowed for God's chosen.

Deirdre cased the town. No luck at the playground, gazebo, or Bay Beach. Not a hint of pink bike or purple hair.

Angie wouldn't tell because of her mother's recurring nightmare. When she was four, she'd lain on the floor in the dark hallway, one cheek pressed into carpet, to see her parents' feet at the corner of the bed that was closest to the door. Her mother was telling her father about a nightmare—of Angie's severed head lobbing from the nursery down the hall like a lopsided bowling ball bleeding on and careening off walls until it thudded into the corner by the hall closet door. Her mother's sobbing. Her father's comforting shushing. The whooshing of blood in her scarlet ears. She never told them she'd heard. She wouldn't tell now.

His mind eclipsed with the sun as it lowered behind the azure water tower on the horizon. The girl with purple hair was still here, her long neck ripe as prey.

On the straightaway toward the library, a dead bird lay in the road. Deirdre aligned the car so the tires wouldn't squish it, but the gray dove, not dead, blinked awake from its sunny nap on the warm macadam. Too late to brake—STAY DOWN! —the dreaded thump. In the rearview mirror, downy under-feathers swirled like a mini-blizzard in August. A dove, of all creatures. Surely a sign, a bad omen. Where *was* Angie? Gone forever, the old fear fulfilled? The rerun of an empty future surged anew and as tangible as the library now passing on her right, where the absence of a pink Schwinn in the bicycle rack struck her as more real than the weathered siding of the building's cedar-shake exterior. She would take a sabbatical at work for a while, or forever. Retire from life, wander disembodied in search of what was lost—from curtain-drawn window to curtain-drawn window to Angie's marine-blue bedroom and its familiar but disturbing visual pollution. Stuffed animals galore. Dusty puppets hanging from hooks in the ceiling, awash with pastel, adhesive-backed, glow-in-the-dark stars. CDs strewn across the carpet coated with lint and dog fur. The puppy dreaming, paws jerking, in a sunspot on the unmade bed. Used tissues stuffed between the bed and wall. Wads of gum-wrapper foil behind the door. Sickeningly sweet incense lying heavy in the air to mask the rot of hidden fruit even the puppy couldn't find. Forgotten dirty laundry crammed under the bed and host to tiny, crescent-shaped worms, some dead, some not.

Love your teen, my ass—the thought squeezed out before she could stop it. She slowed at every side street to scan both ways for an abandoned pink bike. Get a grip, Deirdre argued with herself, Angie has done this a million times before, and all worry is energy wasted. Yet this could be *the* time, she knew, and how could she live with the guilt if she didn't worry, as though worry were a daily tithe, which if withheld exacted the ultimate price. She followed the bends of Ocean Avenue homeward through town toward the Point, no longer a swimming beach due to the annual cost of trucking in sand by the ton, only for the river to steal it again. Deirdre braked hard at the sight of what might be purple hair beyond dune grass waving in the wind.

Muddy Dockers boat shoes approached Angie from behind, slow, measured, quiet save for the barely audible, locust-crisp crunch of parched grass in August lawn.

Angie jumped at the shadow emerging from behind her, birthing from the shoulder of her own shadow, a darker shade of brown than the August lawn. A halo of blinding sun obscured the face, and Angie stared at the feet, the dirty Dockers boat shoes, the navy twill pants sloughing puffs of silt like a dandelion shedding seeds on the breeze, like a whirr of downy feathers from a sacrificial dove.

"Hi, Mom," Angie said. "How'd you get so filthy?"

"Hi, lovey. Just gardening," Deirdre said, glancing down with alarm at the dirty figure she cut. She swatted dried dirt clods and dust from her pants and sat on the bench, neither too near nor too far from her daughter, who, true teen, had forbidden public displays of affection.

Angie tapped her palms and fingertips on the picnic table planks, which had weathered gray and cracked from the damp salty air. Deirdre didn't recognize the tapped tune.

"Is it true that God loved us first so that we could love?" Angie asked, thinking this a good prelude to the postponable yet inevitable discussion of next summer's plans.

From the mouths of babes, Deirdre thought, but she said only, "Yes," not adding what she'd read in the latest issue of the psychology magazine—that hate can never exceed one's capacity for love.

"Can we go to Seaside tonight?" Angie asked.

Deirdre watched the muscles in Angie's forehead hover in anticipation between joy and frown. The raucous noise of the amusement park and its flashing neon lights no longer appealed to Deirdre, but she didn't want scowls to mar her daughter's face. "We'll see if your Daddy is up for a jaunt. We missed our annual carousel ride last year. I'd hate to miss it again."

Angie smiled—whether because she knew she could wheedle her father into most anything, or because she also loved the merry-go-round, or both, Deirdre couldn't be sure.

She imagined stroking her daughter's head, finger-combing her hair, plaiting her purple mane into six braids, which she randomly recalled from high-school Latin was the traditional 'do for brides in ancient Rome. "You're the picture of peace."

"This place *is* peace." Angie squinted, pointed inland. "Look, Mom. The sun looks like an egg yolk."

Shielding her eyes with one hand, Deirdre peered into the brilliance, west, upriver. The sun was setting on the Pine Barrens, dark as charcoal in the distance. Closer, burnt black in silhouette, the tallest Loblolly treetop pierced the gold sac, which dribbled and deflated and purified the now steel-gray river with fire. A weight fell from her chest, yet something wasn't right—her inner child was still missing. Deirdre didn't know whether to mourn. Trembling, she reached to stroke her daughter's hair, which gleamed magenta in the setting sun.

Dying to Dream

After Daddy heads for his Saturday job, Mommy again convinces shrieking Brother, eleven, *smack,* with a kitchen spatula, *smack,* to "RESPECT" her, *smack.* When it's over, you sneak into his bedroom to love sobbing Brother. He's stuck-ity-stuck in self-oozing welts, his I-NOT eyes blind as peeled onions in a dense red sea.

Mommy's rage shifts to Pixie, six, who hides dirty clothes under her bed, where tiny worms curl and die, yuck-ety-yuck. Mommy hurls Pixie's room like vomit, slings "MIS-ALIGNED" books from shelves through air, pages riffling, to *smack* the hardwood floor and slide under the bed, out the door, downstairs. Mommy heaves a chair. Pixie's I-NOT eyes freeze, icicle-tears on her cheeks. Standing behind Mommy on the landing, you watch her arms hate. You could push her—hard—but falling downstairs would hurt Baby, fat inside her.

Mommy turns, still irate. Your turn. *Smack.* "SMART, ARE WE?" she asks, but it's a threat, not a question.

"I not smart a'tall," you say, cheek aflame, "I-NOT." (blank out)

(unblank) While babysitting that night, your sixteenth birthday, you dare hope: pile Pixie and Brother into the Ford and drive up the hill, lickety-split, past streetlamps into stars. Reality bursts your bubble: can't drive. As Responsible Eldest, you stay in the fear with the babies here and yet to come.

Baby, now age two, calls you Mum. On summer mornings, after Daddy's car crests the hill, "real" Mom dispenses *smacks* with the vitamins, guns the Ford to the "post office," and returns at 5:20, letters in hand. She hums, twirls, fondles the newel post and banister. Daddy's home at 5:30 to Mom thumping pots on the stove. You and Daddy smile from I's behind eyes, sensing something. Mom craves mail? Mail? Male? Which male?

Later, babysitting in the dark living room, you design doomed escapes. You conclude you're so ding-dong dumb you should skip college, stand guard at home between siblings and Mom, but you need to get smarter (Mom skipped second grade), get away, get laid—all fodder for guilt in years to come.

Age twenty-seven. Your lungs deflate when your body *smacks* the floor. The current love of your life is throwing a fit you can't understand because he drunkity-drunk raped you last night. You wonder, Shouldn't someone else be having a fitty-fit? Flit to what's for breakfast, Western omelette with cheese?

Days later, you still can't breathe—lungs as useless as pooped balloons. Home at Daddy's, prowling his medicine cabinet, your hand upends bottles like cartons of Jordan almonds. Your tongue catches pastel-orange aspirins, yum-yum, plus countless, multisyllabic, rainbow-pretty pills. Vodka chaser in a Sleeping Beauty cup. Forgot ice. Sink past pain to I-AM, aahhh-see?, so deep ...

Absence of oblivion, hospital room. Hi-I-I, Mom. *Smack.* "YOU NAUGHTY." I-NOT-ee.

Moon-eyed, you tell Mr. Shrinkety-Shrink later, *I did not mean to upset my family.* He doesn't commit you. You don't deserve it—can't commit suicide right, even a second time. When was the first? You can't remember. Remember ice next time. Next time?

Age thirty-seven. The intern's induced labor three times. No dice after forty-two hours. You're the one in a thousand who can't dilate enough, and poor Daughter's stuckity-stuck in fetal distress. They tilt the bed sideways after strappity-strapping you in. Husband's left through a blizzard to "feed the dogs again." You roll your watermelon self out into the ice and let death love Daughter and you, but you're strapped in and doped up, and you croak at the door cracked ajar, *Can someone stop this, PLEASE.* Your Ob-Gyn carves Daughter from your watermelon gut. Morphine kills the cut—sweet.

Two-day-old Daughter naps in your arms, hospital pillows propped all around. You drift into her eyebrows, new memories, peace. You wake at home. Daughter has colic and won't sleep. You shake her. Her tiny fists flail, her face a red sea. You cry "NEVER AGAIN," and you never do shake her again. Amazing, you think, I can do mother love.

Husband says it's over. A younger woman makes him hard. Must be your second (third?) (fifth?) meltdown. If you lose count, do they count?

Age forty-seven, typing Professor's words on a laptop, tappity-tap, your captioning projected for hard-of-hearing students to read. The administrators schedule you in consecutive classes because you say you can't but, martyr-like, do it anyway. What you'd like to type: Brother's dying of AIDs, Pixie's a divorced marriage counselor, and Baby, a teacher, is a closet vigilante. But you have no insights, save stale guilt, so you type other people's words, yakkity-yak, earning bucks for Daughter's future tuition. The Professor then plays auctioneer; you can't keep up and think, *I can't do this anymore,* but somehow say the words out loud. Heads turn, eyes stare. You keep typing, face on fire, relieved you weren't thinking, *Why can't I get flipping laid.*

Age fifty-seven, falling out of love with your FedEx man, who messed with your head. No dignity lost—can't miss what you never had. Fluid drips all around. Ice melting? Tears? Self-ooze? Can't tell, but if love didn't scare you before, it sure scares the cockety-caca out of you now. You forgot infatuation lasts three months and isn't love anyway. It was flirting and fantasy, morphed into *concupiscentia carnis.* Six decades to learn lust isn't love? How absurd can life be? This absurd: Your current quandary—become a hermitess or lounge lizardette?

Movement draws your eyes skyward to choices circling on wings: Clocks, Cocks, Copulate copiously, Conquer fear, Care again, Celebrate life—sip—chug. You want to SOAR. Mr. FedEx man, you think, Thankity-thanks for flirty-fun company destined for crisis while inducing catharsis and freeing hope; please forgive-forget all the disconcerting crap—it wasn't I-AM (how could I-NOT have known?).

You conceive of comfort as you carve your cave clean, craft windows and doors, imagine rain-sweet air hugging aeries. You dream a personal ad: "DWF seeks DWM who thrives on cracked company and flies routinely from Death Valley to Cassiopeia."

Passing On

PART 1. MADAM MACADAM, BIG BAD MAMA

Riled and raucous blue jays dive-bomb the neighbor's cat, which shrieks and yowls like a baby with colic. The cacophony yanks Pearl awake while dawn is still battling gray. Days that begin like this, she thinks with a yawn, always end up being one of THOSE days. The kind of day she blames on cosmic rays or karma or just plain bad luck that seems to fool with her molecules so she wants to crawl out of her skin, leaving it behind like a snake's crisp husk, and slither off to start fresh in a cabin by a lake on wooded acres in Wyoming or Missouri or someplace not here. And neither Mozart nor pancakes nor oak moss incense nor a bubble bath with scented candles can help one of THOSE days. So she contains herself intact in her skin, proud of her calm control while riding out the toothache that kept her up half the night.

[Now Ah done right lettin' her start this tale, but this ain't one THOSE days. This here be the day her calm control—shit, that damn

control's eatin' up her stomach linin'—gonna swallow its tail while bitin' its hiney. Ah knows, cuz that starvin' place inside her gonna shrink so small today it fart me out like a dingleberry pearl—and Ah only gets this here one chance to save her from herself. Ah been waitin' sixteen damn year for just the right moment in time, and this here be it. She a stubborn lady all mess up 'bout damn near everthin'. Her heart right, though, cuz Ah been inside her all this time. What she don't know is today'll git even more piss-poor and then bunches better thanks to cat shit, Madam Macadam, Big Bad Mama—that's me—and a mozzarellie stick. And she dead wrong 'bout pancakes—a thick stack always heps.]

It being one of THOSE days, Pearl doesn't bother to wash up or get dressed. Her bones creak the stiffness out as she limps all the way *snap* downstairs through the living room *crackle,* kitchen, and *pop* back hall to the door to let out and back in Sammie, their white powder-puff dog. Back in the kitchen, Pearl finds no coffee, no tea, no milk. She sighs and pours Rice Krispies, which her knees just suggested, dry into a juice glass. Back in the living room, she plunks herself down with the laptop and stretches out her legs on the sofa. Her goal today is to consider her creative chronicle of a significant episode of family history titled "Letting Go." The story is for Meg, her delightful daughter turned impossible teen, beautiful, spiteful, too independent for her own good—and where *did* she learn it, Pearl wonders, not knowing if she *should* feel guilt but feeling it anyway. As usual while she revises, she takes frequent "brain breaks" by looking out the window, where squirrels chase each other's spasmodic tails and skitter around a tree trunk silhouetted on the white clapboard house next door, where the shadow of Pearl's house shrinks lower and lower as day creeps out of dawn. After a thorough revision of the first draft, she gags at the smell of fresh poop flooding the room.

[Like that. What this sweetsy-poo "poop" crap? If you can call a spade a SPADE, *you can call shit* SHIT. *Maybe then people understan' what the hail she talkin' 'bout.]*

The neighbor's cat, named Cat, has taken a dump in his favorite spot, under the forsythia outside the living room window. Sammie barks at Cat and rushes the window, which is open only a crack to let cool spring air in and to keep Sammie from hurling himself out through the screen. Not because he wants to roll in the crap, like any self-respecting dog should. A lifetime ago, her childhood dog, a sweet black cocker spaniel, rolled three times in one day in the field up the hill freshly fertilized with horse manure, which drove her mother nuts. Pearl and her siblings found their mother's furor hysterically funny—that is, when they weren't close enough to whiff the matted dog, who pranced a high step in her new perfume. Now, of course, Pearl knows she'd have conniptions, too, if she had to bathe Sammie three times in one day.

Sammie stops yapping, and Pearl hears Meg trek heavy-heeled to and from the bathroom and start plucking her bass guitar. Then lawn mowing, leaf blowing, and weed whacking thunder over from across the street, making impossible any semblance of peace as sun starts to warm the morning air. The printer churns out six pages of the second draft while Pearl winds strands of white hair off her neck into a bun. She staples the pages, folds them in thirds, stuffs and seals them in an envelope addressed for now to herself. And she sits. Stares at window space. Mopes. Looks in dread at the envelope in her hands.

The infernal racket outside continues. Yup, one of THOSE days. Pearl yearns for the peace of birds chirping and birch leaves rustling in breeze, but infinitely more she craves connecting with her daughter, now—the way Meg connects with her father—not connecting years in the future once Meg's a mother herself. But why stay where you're not needed, Pearl thinks. That's why she wrote the story as a letter, for Meg to read when Pearl is gone or dead, whichever comes first. Or maybe she'll share the story with Meg sooner, maybe, depending on something, some sign of guidance or intuitive direction.

[Mebe my ass. That where she dead wrong. A chile need know 'bout mother love everday. An' that mistake the icin' on the cake gonna set me free today to make some change aroun' here, an' none too soon, may Ah say, an' Ah do.]

"Meg!" Pearl calls from her nest on the sofa, lined with Sammie on the floor between her and the coffee table, with tissue box, newspapers, books, and computer and printer cables all within arm's reach. No answer, not even a pause as Meg plucks the notes trial-and-error style to, of all things, the "Final Jeopardy" theme, with amp at full volume to compete with the ear-numbing noise across the street—all way too early in the day. Wouldn't "Final Jeopardy's" TV host Alex Trebek be proud, Pearl thinks and then, "So why aren't I?"

['Bout time you ax, you ninny!]

A sudden breeze billows the lace curtains, which Pearl realizes post-sneeze are in dire need of spring, oops now summer, cleaning. "Meg!" No answer. Then Pearl remembers the new name Meg adopted last week. "Murg, Queen of Doom!" Pearl yells from the sofa. Footsteps tag four stairs and thump on the carpeted landing, then repeat the rhythm down to the first floor, where the final jump-thump lands "Murg, Queen of Doom" dangerously close to the coat closet door.

"Sweetie, you're going to smash your head through the door," Pearl pleads. "I wish you wouldn't do that." Toothpick-thin Meg rolls her eyes, just as Pearl did at that age, but Meg adds a slack-jaw mouth and thumps her forehead with an L formed by her thumb and index finger. Pearl has dubbed the gesture Eye Roll #12 (L for "loser" being the 12th letter of the alphabet) to distinguish it from the other slurs. And as usual she suffers in silence.

[That what Ah mean. To hail with patience. Smack her upside the haid, woman. But no, she thinkin': Today's teens have more to worry about. Threats of parents divorcing, AIDs, peer pressure to try drugs and sex, Columbine massacres, World War III nearing fruition in the Middle East, and stuff that really makes them mad: computer screens freezing, the Xbox breaking, DVDs skipping, and losing the cell phone—again. Times have changed. And so, just as the Eskimos built their 125 or so different words for "snow," Meg and her fellow teens are expanding the expressive lexicon just for fun. *Now that's a shitpile o' excuse. Chilluns should always respeck they mothers, an' never let em forget it.]*

"I have three words for you," Pearl prompts.

"Where's Daddy?"

Pearl sighs. "That's only two words, dear. He's still at the conference. So let's go on a Mom and Meg—Murg—outing, like we haven't done in forever. The three words are 'Eagle Rock Diner.' Breakfast."

"That's four. You forgot—Color Guard—dance practice—10 o'clock," Meg says, suddenly light-footed and punctuating her words with pretty, lithesome pirouettes across the room to clean, dry laundry wrinkling in mounds on the antique sofa, where she flops with fake exhaustion, age sixteen going on four. "I'm bored. What's that smell?"

Meg lifts her head from the socks, underwear, and wrinkled T-shirts she didn't fold and put away yesterday, sniffs the air, and shoves her waist-length braid under her nose.

"The damn cat shat under the window again, a good enough reason for a change of scenery, besides all this." Pearl swings her arm to encompass the visual and auditory pollution of living-room clutter and next-door clatter. "You and Daddy spend so much time together—museums, shopping, the city." All thanks to the Electra complex, that age-old wedge between mothers and daughters that cleaves daughters to fathers like compass needles to due north and leaves mothers roaming with goals but no direction.

[Electric complex, mah ass. She slippin' away, an' you set to run off t'other way. Wyomin', woman? What the hail good that do?]

"I miss you. So I'm looking forward to our weekend, just you and I." Pearl fishes out her sandals from the pile of footwear under the coffee table. "Grampa called the other day."

"Which Grampa?" Meg asks with a smirk.

"Well, one is alive, and one is dead. Which one do you think?" Pearl responds, drawn into a game she hates before she realizes it.

"Ha! I have four Grampas, and only one is dead." Meg gloats in her perceived victory.

"My father," Pearl says, in no mood for Meg's orneriness and literality about multiple divorces and step-grandfathers. Maybe there's trout in that lake by the cabin in Wyoming, she thinks—too bad she can't stand to poke hooks through worms.

"Let's go to Panera instead," Meg says, already bored with the grandfather debate.

"No, Eagle Rock Diner." Pearl heads to the kitchen for her purse and keys, which she always places by the wall behind the clutter on the table, which left space for only two to eat there, and she was not one of those two.

"I can't eat before practice, you know," Meg says, crabby still, or again—it's hard to tell these days. She grabs her Guard paraphernalia, and mother and daughter head for the car, stepping over and around "puppy bombs," their family lingo for dog-poop piles.

"You can't have breakfast at 4 this afternoon, sweetie," Pearl yells over the like-clockwork thunder of planes stacked and banking toward Newark Airport, which drowns out the racket next door but not Meg's car-door slam.

[That girl gonna break the hinge. You gonna wait til then smack her upside the haid?]

Pearl hugs the dreaded sharp curves up and around the hill. "Right there is where—"

"—a school bus made you a Sunbird sandwich when you were pregnant with me. Shiz, you've told me a zillion times!" Meg turns away and glares at the forest to her right, her expression reflected in the window.

Of course, Meg has no memory of the bus scratching yellow paint into the right side of Pearl's red Plymouth, while the medial strip scraped to gray metal the other side, and Pearl had clutched her belly to protect her womb and its priceless contents. Pearl switches to a different tack. "When you were three, you asked me, 'Where is my black mommy?'"

[NOW we tunin' in. Go Pearl girl!]

"Say what? Get out!" Meg snaps her face back toward Pearl, who glances over at Eye Roll #1, the legitimate, plain-vanilla, wide-eyed version.

[Cep she don' remember no mo, like chilluns grow up and forget seein' angels.]

"Daddy and I puzzled over that. He thought you were remembering a dream. I thought it was an image from your collective unconscious, Jung style, which actually blends nicely with new findings about mitochondrial DNA, which traces lineage back to a few women, arguably of biblical times, *all* of whom happened to be black," Pearl says.

[Now you talkin'.]

"Hmm." The smooth skin between Meg's eyes folds into a crease.

An idea bubbles up, an idea more tantalizing than the fresco of Wyoming landscape plastered across Pearl's brain. "Listen up. Mom is now mum, or not Mom, depending on your viewpoint. Ah will ansah only ta Madam Macadam, Big Bad Mama," Pearl says, gaze fixed on the road ahead. She doesn't know how she keeps a straight face, doesn't burst into the guffaw that's tickling up from her stomach.

[Hot spit, Madam Macadam! Now Ah's offishul—she said my name. Big Bad Mama!]

"Shiz, are you OK, Mom?" Meg loses her cool and stares at her as though Pearl's mind is oozing out her ear.

Pearl refuses to answer.

Meg corrects herself and chokes on Pearl's new name: "Are you OK, *Madam Macadam?"*

"Don' wase ma tahm axin' no fool questions, Murg, Queen o' Doom," Pearl says. "Ah's you black mama. Ever-body got a black mama inside their haids, jus' gotta reach far nuf in to find her. Inside *you* head, there's a black mama, too."

Meg's mouth drops open.

"Shut that trap befo' mosquitoes bite you tongue an' swell it on up," Pearl says.

Meg snaps her mouth shut, unsure of what is happening yet intrigued by her mother's appealing shift into whacko land. Pearl keeps her eyes on the road, marveling at this new game she's invented with no idea where it will lead. She senses that long-starving place inside her begin to fill, swell with succulent satisfaction, with Big Bad Mama.

[You didn't invent it, but you cookin' with gas!]

Pearl and Meg don't look at each other while parking and getting seated at a booth. Pearl orders pancakes, a surprise to Meg, who orders mozzarella sticks and a grilled cheese sandwich, just as Pearl knew she would. Under the guise of "pick your battles," Pearl doesn't chide. As usual lately, they don't converse. Something tells Pearl to wait as long as it takes for Meg to break the silence. Pearl watches Meg count the eagles, an old pastime revisited but new once again since the grand re-opening. The staff has moved eagle plaques, paintings, and even a dreamcatcher to different homes on new mahogany paneling. Vases and urns painted with eagles now sit atop the sheen of fake-marble counters and on booth tables swirled with black on gray flecked with speckles of gold.

"Since when do you eat pancakes?" Meg asks as the food arrives, but she gets no response.

Pearl delves into her pancakes with one eye on Meg's mozzarella sticks. Pearl weighs her words, yet the somehow primal new role seems familiar. She talks casually to her plate. "You grampa not that ole, but he forget some. He remembah t'othah day some family histohry about you great-great-great gramma Lizbeth. You carryin' her genes, girl, passed to you from you mama. Pass the maple syrup, if you please."

She looks up into Meg's stunned wide eyes.

"Mom, shh, you're very P-I," she whispers, interested nonetheless.

Caught off guard, Pearl slips out of character: "P-I like Magnum, or pi like 3.412? Ah mean, like peecawn pah?"

"No. P-I like in 'politically incorrect'. Could you go for P-C? Please?" Meg pleads, glancing around for eaves-droppers as she passes the syrup. Pearl has already cased the place—no one's seated close enough to offend, and she's talking low.

"If people jus' cep the fact they got they own black mama fo a gardian angel, wouldn' be no P-I now, would they? An' things'd get set right once'n fer all. Nothin' to say, chile?" Pearl asks. Meg's mouth atypically hangs open, not sure how to play this new game.

[Ooh, Miz Mama singin' my song!]

"That Lizbeth she pretty, like her great, great, great granddaughtah, Murg, Queen o' Doom, cep her hair black, like mine useta be. Her huzband Neil's hair red. Tha's where you get you auburn hair. She sing like a bird. Everone fall in love with that girl's voice."

"Is that why I can sing?" Meg asks. She eyes the one mozzarella stick remaining in the middle of her plate. Around the rim, she's lined up the crust edges of her sandwich.

"It's a genetic atavistic trait—I mean, 'course that why you sing," Pearl says with exasperation while inventing and displaying Eye Roll #126, which she can't even describe.

[Shee-it. Get it right. It's with a han' on one hip an' a fryin' pan clutched in t'other like you gonna whomp the daylights outta whatever wanders by.]

"Lizbeth had a baby boy John, and she give up everthin to save that chile. Iffen you think Ah don' have that same mothah love, you dumber than a chickadee nestin' on the groun'. Unerstan' me, girl?"

Pearl glances at the lone mozzarella stick on Meg's plate. Meg cuts it neatly and hands over half on her fork. They share the halves in silence, probing each other's eyes. Pearl sees Meg's awe at a world wider than her navel.

"Big Bad Mama, you're as whacked as Dad," Meg says with an appreciative smile.

Pearl feels a weight in her chest disappear.

Spiro, the restaurant owner, greets them at the cash register. They relive the old days when Pearl, while waiting for coffee to go, would lay baby "Meglet" in her fluffy pink snowsuit on the countertop. Meg loved to look up and watch the ceiling fans spin, there at the diner and at the church where the pastor carried her up and down the aisle for the congregation to admire when she was baptized, and Pearl cried because the pastor was carrying Meg too far away from her.

"You should see her now, in Color Guard," Pearl tells Spiro with pride. "She's a captain, and their team won the Marine's Esprit de Corps Award in Giants Stadium last fall."

Pearl smiles at Meg, who stands an inch taller but whose face has reverted to her toddler-age, embarrassed-shy smile. They all laugh and wish each other well.

Meg opens the diner door for Pearl—a first.

"Thanks, Murg, Queen of Doom," Pearl says, smiling into her eyes, where a myriad shades of green glint in the sun. The chicken pox scar over her right eyebrow has almost disappeared with time. Pearl glows in Meg's rapt attention, which her father had commanded for years now, leaving

Pearl out in the cold. "Feel like driving?" Pearl tosses the keys in an arc to Meg.

"Yes!" Meg squeals with delight and opens the car door for her mother—another first.

"You do me proud, Murg," Pearl says, leaning her head back on the neck rest and shutting her eyes, so Meg knows her mother trusts her to look both ways *and* at the rearview mirror.

Meg hums with the radio and then sings along, "Pave paradise. Put up a parkin' lot."

Paved in sapphire with a tad of macadam. Pearl joins in. Neither of them can hit the bottom note, and they laugh themselves silly at their off-key attempts. As they turn onto their street halfway down First Mountain, a symphony of lawn mowers vibrates the air.

"What about Guard practice?" Pearl asks, surprised.

"I fibbed. Practice was canceled. I'm sorry, my bad, but I'm glad. I'd rather talk with you and Madam Macadam," Meg says, smiling, age sixteen going on thirty, on eight, on sixteen. "You're a whack job, Mom! Like Daddy. You're *bad!"*

Bad—sweeter by far than a paradise of cabin and lake in Wyoming, where the only neighbor is probably a terrorist anyhow. Pearl reaches her hand out the window, feels worry wing away on cool yet warm breeze, and basks in joyous awe at one of THESE rare and glorious days, when a mother, daughter, and Madam Macadam, Big Bad Mama, miraculously converge on the same page.

PART 2. LETTING GO

Dear Meg,

I don't know when I will give you this letter—maybe tomorrow, maybe when you marry, maybe when you deliver your first baby, maybe in a lockbox upon my decease, or whenever I think you will appreciate fully and deeply the concept of mother love. Please pardon my indecision on this point, especially if I misjudge and wait too long.

As a point of reference, however, I almost told you this story yesterday (you were sixteen at the time), but the Southern dialect of Big Bad Mama, Madam Macadam, seized my mouth instead. I wanted so much to impress your teenage self, feel the connection with you that you so freely allow with your dad while shutting me out. Maybe Madam had been hiding inside me just waiting for that special moment to appear. Maybe she was an ancient elemental voice. Maybe she was a streak of lunacy. Maybe a Southern dialect relating an Irish tale seemed too absurd. Maybe she came out because it was premature to share the tale. Maybe a combination of these speculations—who knows? In any case, you were so delighted with how "whacked" I/she was (what a compliment!) that I didn't want to break the spell.

Do you remember Madam Macadam? If so, you will recall that on a typical day, you answered only to "Murg, Queen of Doom" and interpreted any mention of your youth as accusation. You needed me less than I needed you, but when you did need me, you really, really, like, *really* did. Your eyes glowed with daydreams of friends, boys, Color Guard, and school. You spent your "quality time" mostly without Daddy and I—we sat at home fearing the empty nest. I couldn't bear for you to leave but couldn't say no when you asked to borrow my car. You had no time to write a thank-you note but found hours to polish your nails and make up your face, which never needed embellishment. Your natural beauty glowed. You wrote emails with less English than smiley faces, exclamation points, "lol," "lmao," and "ha." And, of course, "so-cha," my favorite of all your made-up words because when you said it, your face was at peace with the world. In your eyes, I saw innocence passing but not yet lost, and I couldn't stop the loss to come.

I have loved every stage of your life, even parts of your crazy teens, believe it or not (Xanax helped with the other parts; don't knock it—you may need it someday, too). You may blame me for withholding the enclosed information until now, but "I'm the mother." Remember how that phrase drove you nuts? Just a tease, my dear, for old time's sake (bad mama—sorry). I can imagine you as a mother, finding ample opportunity to use my last-resort line while comprehending finally the depth of a mother's love.

You descend from strong-willed people, sweetie, such as your great-great-great grandfather, Neil McClain, and, in particular, his wife Elizabeth, whose sacrifice ensured your life and mine. She is in your blood and your children's, if you are so blessed by now. When Big Bad Mama mentioned "Lizbeth" in passing to you yesterday, your response was "Cool!" Here is Elizabeth's story.

While the potato crop failed three times between 1845 and 1848, whoever could leave Ireland did in order to escape what would become known as the Great Famine. At age 18, Elizabeth (last name unknown or perhaps Logan or Lougan) was the youngest, healthiest, and most timid member of her family, whose small middle-class fortune meant little when little food could be grown or bought. Her family paid all to save one: the ship passage for Elizabeth on the *Hiram,* bound for America in 1845, was their ultimate investment in futures. At the cold, raw waterfront, Elizabeth and two cousins—her mother stayed at home, too weak to travel—huddled in the finality of hugs that when broken would break their hearts, too. When the *Hiram* sailed from port, onlookers wept as they watched their hopes sail toward horizon and future. Elizabeth, like the others, waved sobbing at the rail as home shrank into distance and memory.

The national bond between those aboard—culture, legend, song and dance, impoverishment—was sealed further, despite feisty temperaments, by congeniality, hunger, and grief. The émigrés, fleeing to save their lives and thus prolong their lineages, told familial variations on the same theme: a dirge of starvation, death, and lime-sprinkled grief piled on grief in mass graves. Elizabeth watched new friendships begin, be tested, and, if found lacking, change during the first week. By the second week, people clustered in the same groups—on deck in fair weather, or below when it stormed—but not with Elizabeth, who isolated herself in corners, shy and terrified, never before separated from the familiarity of her kin.

During the second week, red-haired, bushy-bearded Neil McLean, seven years Elizabeth's senior, sought to comfort her when he found her huddled in the hold, head down, hiding streams of tears behind long dark locks. Lonely desperation helped her overcome shyness and fear, and she welcomed Neil's solace, not only then but time and again. His cousin Alexander was a font for Neil when Elizabeth's sorrow sucked Neil dry. Elizabeth eventually offered comfort in return, which forged a bond of mutual appreciation and friendship that opened a door in Neil for attraction and, more, desire, although he would never speak of such a thing to the young and innocent Elizabeth.

They appeared more often than not as a threesome on deck, Alexander in tow, propriety at the fore, but even the children aboard recognized, and mimicked, Neil's shy and glowing gazes, which Elizabeth found herself returning against her better nature while vaguely wondering what drove her better nature.

On an overcast day, when Neil asked about Elizabeth's family and home, she cried so hard she couldn't utter a word. The first wet drops of a storm plopped on the dark deck planking, hung in Neil's beard, and beaded beside Elizabeth's tears on her green wool shawl. He urged her below deck, but she wouldn't budge because the rain somehow linked her through the sky with home. He shushed and held her in the downpour until thunder vibrated the air, at which he lifted and carried her below deck out of danger. This intimacy—his touch and concern—as well as his manly strength, opened the door to Elizabeth's heart, and she consciously stopped resisting the resistance of her better nature.

Elizabeth clutched Neil's neck and buried her head in his chest, which smelled of wet wool and the salty sea. He tried to distract what he interpreted as her fear with his history, the story of the McLeans. He began in reverse order, with the unexpected news that he'd stocked many barrels of smoked salmon in the cargo hold of the *Hiram.* Elizabeth's dark brown eyes opened wide in amazement—so the McLeans were not poor at all. She hung on his words, hoping her attraction to him would not be sullied by greed.

The McLean men caught salmon on tiny Carrickarede Island, connected to the mainland by a rope bridge, suspended eighty feet above a rocky chasm, a narrow strip of sea, and four caves below. Three of the caves extended deep into the cliff and were large enough to contain a boat. The fourth cave was shallow and resembled a Gothic arch carved by nature or God and certainly too majestic for man's creation. Every echo in the caves was spectacular, and a bugle call near each cave re-echoed on a different key and formed a chord of inexpressible beauty that never left one's soul once heard. Neil and Alexander, son of Margaret and William, were born and raised in Glenstaughey (pronounced *glen-STUCK'-eh*), County Antrim, where they atypically divided their labors between two professions: salmon fishing and raising sheep on pastureland that reached inland toward mountain glens and dropped off at the sea in stone cliffs facing Rathlin Island and, only a dozen miles away, the Scottish Mull of Kintyre. Elizabeth had never heard of Glenstaughey, understandably because it wasn't a town, just the two hundred acres that constituted town land in the parish, of which the only village was tiny Ballintoy.

Elizabeth's sobbing stopped somewhere mid-story, and she raised her head to watch his lips form words.

"A giant shared our land, doncha know," Neil said.

Elizabeth's eyes opened wide, and Neil continued. About eight kilometres northwest of the McLean homestead loomed the Giant's Causeway, a geologic landmark Elizabeth had heard of but never seen. She marveled at the movement of Neil's beard as he described the forty thousand basalt blocks that in ancient times had erupted as lava from the ocean bed and cooled with geometric precision in chaotic groups: large cubes and hexagonal blocks rubbed smooth by surf along the low coast, as well as closely packed rectangular columns that rose in time-weathered steps to a height of forty feet at the northernmost sea wall. According to oral history, the benevolent giant, Finn MacCool, had heaved the basalt blocks from shore to form a stairway from the Irish Sea to the Straits of Moyle, the narrowest expanse of the North Channel, in order to do battle with the threatening Scottish giant, Bendonner. Neil's eyes twinkled, inviting comment.

"Get on wi yeh," Elizabeth said, unsure if he was having fun with her. But her eyes twinkled back and then disappeared in shyness under lowered long lashes, which mesmerized Neil.

He lifted her tresses away from her face and lay them on her back. "Tis true," he said.

"Naught," she said, "tis but legend."

"Listen ta the focts fairst, missi—then joodge," he said, his blue eyes, red moustache, and full lips curling into three smiles.

Similar basalt columns were exposed along hillocks on McLean meadows, which Elizabeth perceived as a sign. She asked Neil several times over the course of their sea voyage to repeat the description, which fleshed out the appealing image of the stone steps and coincidentally, as it eventually occurred to her, her steep climb from a dire past to a hopeful yet impossible-to-imagine future.

In time, Elizabeth could speak of her family without too many tears. Neil seemed to hold all her words dear, and her confidence grew, little by little. She was raised in a thatch-roof cottage on her family's small farm in Culleybackey, borough of Ballymena, southwest of Neil's county. The thick stone walls of the cottage were held together with a lime-and-water plaster, and the family threw a party for the neighbors who helped with the annual repair and painting—several coats of whitewash—before their boots thudded in unison, bouncing the wide-planked floor with dance inspired by fiddles, ballads, Irish whiskey, and moonlight.

On the *Hiram,* when Elizabeth's supply of dried and smoked rabbit ran out, Neil and Alexander saw that she did not want for food—discreetly, of course, lest shipmates learn of and raid the McLean's stock of smoked salmon. Shortly thereafter, in the ship's hold, the most private spot for that time of day, Neil proposed marriage. Elizabeth thought of her mother. Her dear mother who, offering a lifetime of advice in the days before the *Hiram* left port, favored making a suitor wait a day for a "yeh." Her ailing mother, too weak to gather her own wiry gray tresses in a bun. Her poor mother, probably already dead, her open eyes fixed forever on a vision of her daughter's wedding.

Elizabeth accepted Neil's proposal on the spot. Mid-afternoon, two days later, while the sun teased steam from the deck, wet from a morning downpour, a Presbyterian pastor conducted the marriage ceremony for Neil and Elizabeth. A sweetly maternal woman had woven Elizabeth's hair around seagull feathers, the only adornment available, collected by a child at the wharf before the *Hiram* sailed from Ireland. The ceremony naturally segued into drinking and dancing, a welcome relief for exhausted passengers who were sick of their grief. The McLeans rationed extra portions of their food supply and had enough Bushmills whiskey to fill empty mugs until twilight. Even the children got drunk.

Only then did Neil learn Elizabeth's secret. She sang ballads pure as an Irish stream and coaxed notes to hover over the deck like mists over glens. Every night thereafter, passengers pleaded with her to perform. Youthfully shy at first, but with Neil's encouragement, she sang them to their new home, sometimes mournful, sometimes gay, but always with the voice of mother Ireland. All the passengers fell a little in love with her.

The *Hiram* docked at Philadelphia, where the McLeans were obliged by immigration officials to change their name to McClain. Fortune met the McClains shortly thereafter. The Schuylkill River canal system had flourished for twenty-five years, and the owner of a fleet of canal barges sought a buyer so he could retire. Neil and Alexander were soon co-owners of the Harmony Canal Barge Company. Alexander ran the business while Neil built a new home of pine in Port Kennedy, Pennsylvania. It was a small two-story box of a home, but it was theirs—as well as Alexander's until he married and built a house two doors down.

Elizabeth and Neil settled into marriage, and marriage settled into routine. Neil was home every night for a fortnight, then away for a fortnight as barge captain, riding 100 miles up the canal's staircase of locks and dams to the coal mines in the Allegheny Mountains at the end of the line. In towns along the way, he delivered lumber and goods manufactured in the Delaware Valley. On the return trip, he delivered Allegheny coal by the ton, which fueled factories en route to Philadelphia and the Industrial Revolution. The barge company was the first to provide passenger service. Neil managed the payroll. He negotiated the best price with immigrant boat repairmen, who flocked to canal locks, where new towns sprang up seemingly overnight with small homes, a general store, tavern, and church. He traded goods with stable hands and blacksmiths, who cared for the mules and horses that lumbered along tow paths to haul the barges. Occasional flooding—which required extensive repairs—drought, and freeze did not set back the company finances as much as they had feared. Life was good.

Elizabeth loved their new home from the start. To please her, Neil had built a large hearth and a one-and-a-half door, even though a Dutch door could have been ordered pre-made from carpenters in Philadelphia. She loved to latch open the full door whenever the weather was warm and dry, so the breeze swept in above the half door and waffled the window curtains she had sewn from a bolt of beige homespun. With the remaining fabric, she sewed a shawl and a long-sleeved dress with a gathered skirt that reached the floor. When Neil was away, she wore this as her work dress to save wear and tear on her other two gowns. She planted and tended vegetable, fruit, herb, and flower gardens, which thrived on Pennsylvania sun and soil and her passionate care. She took in sewing, hoping to lessen the ache of Neil's two-week absences, and she earned a modest income. Neil always asked for seconds when she cooked barley soup or mutton stew. Typical of the times, their first two children Eliza and Andrew died, 5 months apart in 1858, but Elizabeth was with child again. Life was good.

John L. McClain entered the world on April 3, 1860. His thatch of red hair rivaled the charming unruliness of Neil's. John cooed and smiled when Elizabeth sang of the glens of Antrim, and he loved to pat her lips with one chubby hand and grip her hair with the other. He was healthy. The family thrived. Life was good.

On the evening of January 29th, 1861, while Neil was en route north to the coal mines of the Allegheny Mountains, Elizabeth was carrying baby John and a lantern down the stairs of their home. She tripped and stumbled, dropping the lantern, and her dress caught fire. As she flailed at her skirts and tried to hold John up out of harm's way, the dropped lantern set the floorboards burning. The rest of the wood house flamed ablaze in seconds.

She resisted the instinctive impulse to hug her child to her breast, seized the heating knob of the inner door, and heaved the heavy wood aside. With a giant, stone strength, without so much as a kiss to his head, she flung her child out the half-door. Watched his flailing body arc from view, just as her cousins in Ireland had watched her sail over the horizon. Elizabeth burned to ash and shards of charred bone. Neighbors, alerted by smoke and fire-balls thundering through doors, rescued John unharmed before walls and beams could collapse on him.

As the flames engulfed her, Elizabeth could not know that she would receive no gravestone, no burial plot other than the smoking mound of her American home, no obituary, no death certificate. Nor that Neil would be murdered in a payroll robbery less than three years from then, a decade before railroads put the canals out of business. That Alexander's widow Jane would raise John and keep his mother's memory alive for him. That John would keep the bare essence of Elizabeth's memory alive for his children. That her great-grandson would pass on by word of mouth what by then had become a mere snippet of ancestral trivia. Nor that her great-great-granddaughter would fictionalize Elizabeth's story years after finally finding Neil's gravestone—in the cemetery at First Presbyterian Church of Port Kennedy, the only building and grounds left in what once was the canal town of Port Kennedy, the rest of which was bulldozed under in 1980 after the National Park Service seized the land through eminent domain in order to expand Valley Forge National Park.

Neil's gravestone, barely legible 150 years after its carving, reads:

Sacred to the memory of Neil McClain
A native of Glen Stoughey, County Antrim, Ireland
who departed this life suddenly September 26, 1864
in the 44th year of his age

In sum, my precious Meg, had I known her story earlier, you might have been named Elizabeth. She is alive in your blood. Please keep her alive in your words as well—pass her story on, up the staircase of hope that each generation builds into the future. You already know your gift of song comes from Elizabeth's genes. Should her poignancy, however, remain merely "Cool!" to you, contemplate deeper levels when you're ready—that your singing talent is a secondary gift from Elizabeth, without whose supreme sacrifice we would not exist. I pray that her song swells your heart to giant heights, sweet daughter of mine, sweet joy of my life.

All my love,
Mom (a.k.a. Madam Macadam, Big Bad Mama) ☺

How Beautiful Without Shoes

MARK 7:32-34: They brought to him a deaf man ... and he spat ... and said ..., "Be opened."

JOHN 9:1-7: ... he saw a man blind from birth. ... He spat ... and made mud with the saliva and said, "Go, wash in the pool of Siloam."

I

On the bank of a river, a fox (and what *is* a fox, really?) is resting his back on an ancient banyan tree when underwater movement draws his eyes down from white-swirls-on-azure to azure-ripples-on-lapis-brown. He stares into the depths of nature's spittle at what looks like a fish (and what *is* a fish, really?).

A fish has been swimming in circles for so long and is so tired she doesn't know which way is upstream or down. She sees a fox but is so dizzy she does not trust that she could possibly see from underwater a fox on the shore. She sees red fur again ... and again. She stops circling to peer at a fox. He casts a line, the hook baited with words, which float, dappling the surface of the water. She shimmies up toward light to marvel at the words, familiar words (his or hers?), whose meanings waffle as they rock on the waves.

The fish shies, turns away, gazes back at the fox she is apparently seeing, who appears to be gazing back at her. She is hooked. She pierces her mouth on the hook baited with words and bleeds but does not mind—be it fright or a lifeline, it is new, it is now. He reels her in, but only so far. So it can't be hunger, or can it? What is this strange thing?

She thinks, *If I were a beautiful young woman, not a fish, I would wade to shore and say, "Wordplay. Nicely played, sir. Masterfully played, Sir Fox."* And she would bow her head in awe and humility and maybe peer with desire. But she is not a beautiful young woman. She is a fish. She swims near and flicks her tail, spritzing him with water. He spits on her.

II

In the middle of a living room, John Fox and Jane Fish (and who *are* they, really?) gaze into each other's eyes and smile. Their fingers intertwine. Jane's gaze drops to his lips, soft and supple, kissable, the portal of his treasured words. Vertigo lures her tingling lips to the abyss.

She blinks. She is chained to a black furnace in a sooty basement with an antiquated coal chute. She spits on the furnace, and it disappears. She spits on her chains, and they disappear. (And what *is* the essence of spit, really, but water, which is mere water?)

Jane blinks and rematerializes in the living room with John. Her gaze falls to his parted lips. His hands fly out of hers, flail for a banister to grab. She rescues his hands, presses them to her breasts. Her right breast is too small. He does not seem to mind, but he does not say what she wants to hear, *You are a Picasso sketch in true perspective.*

Furnace flames burn and rise. Scientific fact: heat rises. Musing together, they smile into each other's eyes and lean in with open lips. Should she share secret insights or kiss this mad dream of love? Will her lips know what to do?

III

Brain and self-oozing Heart (and what *are* organs, really?) float free on Van Gogh swirls of azure and lapis-brown, no longer bound by sinew, flesh, and bone. From height and depth in this murky swirl of void, they reflect on the debacle to learn something, anything.

Brain is chastising Heart, "My lady, lips may sculpt exquisite words, but they also spurt flirtatious diddly-squat that accelerates desire and addles me—to wit, your brain."

"I am not owned by intellect. You are mine," Heart says.

"Only when addled," says Brain, "when without my protection, you err—i.e., there was no love; now you are dead to him. The price of possession."

"Love is dead," Heart says.

"*Love* and *dead* are four-letter words," says Brain. "So are *fuck* and *holy,* and that's the crux of the problem, isn't it? Can't pursue both without losing one. Could you ever manage either well?"

"Time to find out, I suppose, one way or the other." Heart sighs, undulating the void.

"So what are you waiting for?" goads Brain. "Go scout out prospects at the pub, or find another fishing hole and focus on your soul."

"Sole?" Feet sing "O Sole Mio" in two-part harmony.

"It's now or never," Soul interrupts, singing tenor.

"Feet and Soul, you're flat—shoo," says Brain. "Now, dear Heart. Focus. Pub or fishing hole?"

"Both," Heart whispers, pulsing faintly.

"To fuck *is* holy," Cunt chimes in late to clarify Brain's pronouncement to Heart. [1]

"Oh my god, a twit," says Brain.

"You mispronounced it," says Sphincter.

"You're talking out your ass," says Brain. "Now blow—meaning scram."

"Is there a god in all this?" Heart cries, skipping beats.

"I am—" Cunt begins.

"Blasphemy," says Brain.

"—the mother of all children," Cunt finishes.

---

[1] BRAIN: "Dear reader, in spite of the author's objections, *I,* Brain, am adding this explanatory footnote."

FEET: "*Foot*-note? Whoa, we have nothing to do with this."

BRAIN *(ignoring Feet)*: "Specifically, the word 'Cunt'—clearly a four-letter word—is perceived and used in the United States as profane, insulting, disgusting, taboo, and arguably the most vile word in the English language. Most Americans don't realize that the word is used with no negative or derogatory connotation in much of Europe and elsewhere, where the word is simply a physical description of the female genitalia, in part or in toto. The word appears here in that unsoiled sense."

EARS AND NOSE: "Scents? We have nothing to do with this either."

AN EDITORIAL VOICE IN THE DARKNESS: "Dear reader, please ignore this footnote, which appears without the consent of the author. My sincere apologies for any inconvenience."

"We see what you mean," Eyes say.

"Does anyone smell fish?" Nose asks.

"More importantly," Elbows ask, "why are we swimming across the Milky Way?"

"Who let a funny bone in the joint?" Sphincter asks. "We all are floating on a meniscus of mercury in a rectal thermometer."

"No, the organs perch in us," Lungs say, "and this interior monologue is making us wheeze."

"*Mono*-logue? At least we can count," Hands say, waving to Heart.

"Greetings, friends," Heart addresses the gathering organs. "Setting aside for a moment where this place is, does anyone know why 'we' are so ... so—disconnected?"

"Jane Fish has come unglued, as they say, resulting in my literal interpretation of the anatomy form of prose fiction," says Brain.

"That's convoluted," Shoulder Blades say. "This is a parallel universe."

"An outdated notion," Eyes say. "Look ahead—join us in the now almost-future."

"Hear here," Ears say. "But couldn't it be an alternate reality?"

"Maybe Jane is dead," Feet say, "since we can't feel ourselves."

"Ow," Breasts say.

"Pardon," Shoulder Blades say.

"Are we the only ones asleep here?" Feet ask.

"Will Jane remember this ... this—" Heart searches for *le mot juste*.

"Chaos?" Brain fills in for Heart. "Humans prefer to forget lost-love nightmares."

"Or is life the nightmare?" Heart inquires.

"Dear, dear Heart," says Brain. "Life is a dream. *This* is reality."

"Are we hearing you correctly?" Ears ask.

"Help. Dizzy. Faint," Heart blurts, wobbling.

"Now Heart," says Brain. "Calm down. Listen up. To the point: You cannot want *both* to fuck and be holy—*both* is a four-letter word."

Heart recovers a faint beat but sighs. "True, true, nothing left to do but redefine and hope."

"Yes?" Hope asks. "So glad you remembered me."

"Too crowded in here for anyone's tastes?" asks Brain.

"I will not rise to the occasion," sniffs Nose.

"There's food?" Tongue asks.

Brain spits with exasperation into the swirling void.

The swirling spit splats on Eyes. "Now we're all wet."

"Oh, my, so am I," Cunt says.

"What is this—some kind of joke?" asks Brain. "Who authorized this parody?"

"Pair o' what?" Ears ask.

Eyes glance at Breasts.

"Don't blame us. We're uplifting," Breasts say.

"*We.* We've heard it five times now, and that makes *six*," Ears say.

"How nice," Hope says. "Inclusion."

"Did someone say *sex?*" Cunt asks.

"Parody? Seems more like a Menippean satire to us," Elbows say.

"Oh my God." Brain spits again into the swirling void.

The organs cringe and wait. Silence reigns. At the speed of light, Hope and Soul drift apart to edges of the void and alternate hefting it upside down and around.

"Goodie, double Dutch," Feet say. "And the feeling is coming back."

One Hand claps. One Eye winks.

"You're ALL bent," says Brain.

"A-L-L—three letters—like *fox*," Hope says.

"No, my dear, *fucks* is a five-letter word," Ear and Cunt correct in unison.

"You're all the epitome of four-letter words," growls Brain.

Heart sputters. "My dear Brain, *word* is a four-letter word. *Really.*"

"Shit," says Brain.

"If you say so," Sphincter says.

"NO," they all shout, spitting on one another.

The void of azure and lapis-brown whirls into a vortex of swirling spit in which the organs merge, parts of one blurred whole joined by sinew, flesh, and bone.

SHALL IT BE MALE OR FEMALE? A bass voice pounds the void like storm-flung hail on kettle drums.

"Female, please," Cunt says and then blushes fur red. "Sorry to be so direct. It's a matter of survival—me, humanity. Are mixed motives OK?"

"May she be sweet and fair?" Eyes ask. "And God Almighty beautiful, to take the breath away?"

"Shut the fuck up," shouts Brain.

Silence rains, diluting the spit.

"Now. Who are YOU, Entity Who Speaks in All Caps?" asks Brain. "And if *you're* here, why am *I* here?"

I AM. The words reverberate as echoed thunder throughout the void.

"Which question are you answering?" demands Brain.

"There's the rub," Cunt says.

At which the void stops swirling so abruptly that the head of the blurred whole slides into its vagina and rams the cervix, where melted self, slick as lubricating jelly, has advantages. Vaginal muscles massage, contract, push. And, *pop,* out *you* slide (and who *are* you now, really?).

"I am Word," you say.

You writhe rise soar dive writhe rise align.

IV

The water in this river is mountain-snow sweet, and you sip, step ashore cleansed, naked, dripping fertile words on old earth awaiting seed. Descaled, deferred, humbled, hungry, you hanker without object until your eyes spot spongy grains on a path into the woods. You stoop, peer closer. Sprinkled on a swath of moss, little pieces of bread point the way from past to future. Shafts of sun thick with motes break through the dense canopy, exposing objects you now recognize. Fern. Redwood. Pine. Spruce. More crumbs. You follow. Crumbs of memory. *Faure's Requiem.* Rousseau jungles. Pints of Guinness. Salted, smoked, and fried sole (and what *is* sole, really, you wonder). All available for sensuous consumption—somewhere. You remember: at the local Internet café/gin mill. The one off Main Street. The only waterfront building of pointed stone. The "Bowssen Inn"—named for the dunking stool at the bulkhead out back and the medieval miracle cure for all that ailed women via submersion, clothed and shod, in icy waters until healing and wholeness occurred or, in zealots' hands, hypothermia or asphyxiation. You shudder, which is when you smell fragrant white pine and turn to a low bough where a lone bread crumb reminds you the inn's under new management, is no longer the "Bowssen Inn" at all. Now it's called "The Fox and Fish," a pub that promises a miracle cure of a different kind. You recall the red fox on the plaque out front, which swings creaking in breeze that sweeps cobblestoned streets, the dunking stool out back long gone. Deep in the dim of the forest now, luminous bread crumbs lead you to a clothesline between trees. You help yourself to jeans and a white T-shirt, relish the air-soft cotton on what feels like a fin on each shoulder blade, stuff pockets full of four-letter words for "just in case," pin one over your heart and one in your hair, scoop up bread crumbs that melt on your tongue, savour barefoot the moss path back to the river—aim upstream for town, people, angels, sun-warmed stone under your soles.

PART THREE

The Firmament

Galatea, I:[1] Fifth Eye in the Fall

Galatea, I,
Unearthed in turbary by a Traveler's tread—
Near the pillars of the earth (the world without end);
Ocean; green cliffs to land, love, and play Lady play;
And blue sky to fly.
Oh my, and Om eye.
—Pleoneveia, *Somniare Perferre Canere Saltare,* lines 1-6

---

[1] Each of the five panels (major sections) in "Galatea, I" refer to one of the five movements, or opuses, of Beethoven's Sixth Symphony, *The Pastoral.* Readers who desire a multimedia experience—reading while listening to the music to which the artists in the story are listening—may go online to access a free streaming music website, such as: https://content.thespco.org/music/compositions/symphony-no-6-pastoral-ludwig-van-beethoven/
In this text, the identifying information about each movement appears underlined for easy reference near the beginning of each panel. *Note:* The characters do not listen to the movements in order.

The First Panel

> Why feud when a lasting concord can be forged,
> Secured now and forever with a marriage pledge?
>
> —Pleoneveia, *Somniare Perferre Canere Saltare,* lines 846-847

With props and Jane in place, the studio set is precisely staged and lit per the photos from the previous session, displayed full screen in the slideshow on John's laptop. The computer appears eerily futuristic near the Renaissance set surrounded by hanging swags and backdrops, stretched canvasses, palettes, easels leaning askew on walls, scattered pigment tubes.

Mid-set, Jane watches John's mustache curve into smile, the focus of his eyes sliding into freely creative drift, so familiar to her after only three sessions. Intrigued by his talent, she delights in the intensity of his pleasure. Her eyelids drop, and she slips with ease into her pose "zone": her sense, based on his art, of his sense of the scene. *Dawn floats at first blush through the eastern side of a windowed studio, stopping springtide at an artist, oils on canvas, and a woman posing nude before burgundy drapes. Angled white silks reflect the sunrise softly, glaze her smooth curves. Muted spotlights cast warmth on private shadows, add sheen to dark tresses swirling to her forearm, graze her left breast, brighten her dainty hand with fingers fixed, tapping music by ear along her cherubic cheek. "Scene by the Brook," Second Movement of Beethoven's* Pastoral, *swells through a gold drape along the western walls.* What is it about John that intrigues her so? She doesn't want to acknowledge the question, her wedding to another only five weeks away.

"Jane, dear, I know it's early, but closed eyes won't do. Blink once hard, open your eyes wide, then relax. … Now do it again. … Good."

Jane fuses her thoughts with his vision, melds mind with body in the classical feminine S-curve, sees herself in the final painting during the act of its creation. Air dust suffuses the low sun on her body, smooth, toned with ripe youth. The sun gleams April blue on a narrow strip of hair, ringing her head with a partial halo. Scenting the room is full-bloom spring wisteria, its drooping lavender clusters in silhouette on the now peach-streaked sky. She floats motionless in his eyes, on the canvas, in time, on the wall (a museum's?) where the painting will hang long after they're dead.

John stares at her around the easel, brow furrowed, and taps the wood end of a paintbrush on his dark, close-cropped beard. Jane holds the pose, aware of magic in every detail around them. He picks a sloe from a bowl of fruit on the table, eyes it, sniffs it, bites it. She tastes it. The Second Movement of the *Pastoral* ends in a hush, and the silence is broken only by a distant waterfall. In a dark bush outside, she knows, a nightingale thrush tends her first clutch; her mate warbles *good night* in fluty trill and reedy staccato. The muted waterfall thunder and nearby birdsong intertwine in a double helix of music.

"Damn. Where's the remote control?" John mutters.

She doesn't answer, doesn't move, doesn't blink. She's learned her lesson. When he asked her last week why she worked at Turkey Hill Farmer's Mart instead of Studio Gallery 357, where she could utilize her art history degree, and she fumbled at an explanation involving maximizing income to cover wedding costs, he cut her off so abruptly she choked in alarm, and he had to "waste time" reposing her. Perhaps he was just moody that day.

He strides toward the DVD/CD player in the western corner. The gold drape muffles his voice, "I hope you don't mind hearing the 'Second' again."

While Jane hears the click of the button John presses, she wonders idly if he is independently wealthy. He owns the studio and its grounds, including the barn out back, and apparently is not compelled to work full time, doesn't mind being "only" an adjunct professor. Yet he says he can't afford to pay for a model. It occurs to her then that she knows little about John. And only a bit less about him than she knows about her fiancé, who has been annoying of late, condescending, quick to find fault with her and admonish. She assumes his behavior is just pre-wedding jitters. John doesn't duck low enough on his way back, and the drape musses his hair. She stifles a giggle.

"Are you absolutely sure you don't mind painting your version from my easel?" John asks. "I know you can't afford a model—who can these days—but I don't want you distracted by my interpretation."

Jane holds the pose. He might be testing her again. She doesn't want to lose this job, even though it's not for pay, just a barter—her modeling for use of his studio and supplies.

"Cat got your tongue, girl?" John asks, even though she's no longer a girl. She can sense his impatience to resolve this side note of business and get back to the paint.

Jane turns to face him. "You said never to break pose."

The flicker of shock on his face turns to an understanding smile, a tad too paternal for her tastes—they're both in their thirties, though at different ends of the decade. "I did indeed," John says. "Let me clarify my definition: 'unless otherwise specified'. How is that, my dear?"

Jane's eyes open wide. No one, not even her fiancé, has ever shown such patience with her literal side. "Duly noted, kind sir," she says, smiling shyly, an old habit from her teens that she never could break.

"I like that: 'sir.' May I call you 'madame'?" John asks, smiling shyly as well in spite of himself.

Jane is amazed to see a flush rise above his beard. "I'd like that very much, sir."

Then she blushes, too, catches herself too late, sees in her mind's eye the jealous face of her fiancé when she told him she posed nude for John because she'd thought in her churched, Pennsylvania farm-girl naïveté that secrets could wound love. She wonders now if she is flirting with John, or he with her. It doesn't matter; this must stop. "I'd prefer to paint from the scene photos on your laptop and refer to your canvas as a guide—as my teacher in your absence, as it were," Jane says, all business. "But only if you don't mind."

A part of John does mind. He feels a pang in his throat that she prefers to learn not *only* from his art—he's more experienced after all, by almost ten years. But he brushes the hurt aside; she clearly has her own vision—he's seen it already in her roughs—and he wants to encourage it. "Consider it done. Oh, I had a duplicate studio key made for you. I'll leave it on your purse." He fishes for it in his pocket.

"The remote's under it," Jane calls as he disappears behind the easel.

"What?" he asks.

She waits. His hand, twirling the remote, emerges beside the easel.

"Sorry, sir," Jane says, flushing again, not sure why.

He flashes her a thankful smile beside the twisting remote and then grins, points the remote at her, clicks, and commands, "Pose."

And just like that she turns her head, adjusts the tilt, relaxes her lips, opens her eyes in pleasant surprise.

"We work well together, madame, don't you think?" he asks, not expecting an answer, already lost in the paint.

She tries to nudge her thoughts back into the pose "zone," but she doesn't want to stop pondering his pensive smile—in spite of his random gray moods—and the mesmerizing twinkle of his blue eyes when he laughs, his dark hair curling at neck and brow, the way he rolls up his shirt sleeves just far enough to hint of manly biceps and triceps, the measured manner of his stride, almost a Russian Mummenschanz dancer's glide with muscles rolling ever so smoothly, the way he talks with a mixture of accents, making him an Everyman in a sense—her enjoyment of all these things. *Where were you born?* She cannot ask mid-pose, of course. Maybe she'll ask him later, after the session.

He drops a lopsided tube of pigment, which flops across the unfinished wood floor before stopping abruptly at an uneven plank. He goes to retrieve it. Ever so slightly, she shifts her eyes to watch his ass return to the easel. The word "ass" doesn't fit the setting. She edits herself into the woman in the painting-to-be who is more refined and when pressed whispers "gluteus." At which she feels something telltale shift in her chest, senses a new door open wide in her brain that she doesn't want to close and through which she admires and wishes for more of John's wisdom and kindness, his humor, his company. But she, like everyone, knows not to mix business with "that," and she has a semi-stable fiancé, blond with hazel eyes, and John wears a ring. So she buries the newborn desire, focuses her pose in toto on John's artistic vision.

She feels her cheeks glow peach with the rising sun, her nose long and narrow, dividing the fruit. Her eyes, black as sloes, aim at the back of the easel, her head tilted as if admiring the distant sunrise. Dangling from a Grecian urn above her left shoulder, ivy swells in growing sunlight from dark to green. A leaf drifts to her thigh.

John appears around the easel. She does not change her gaze. Frowning, he walks to the platform and adjusts a fold of drape, tilts the reflecting screen to shed more light on her breasts and pink nipples.

After nursing your first child, those nipples will tan, John thinks. *Has anyone told you that yet?* He wants to ask, to fondle those nipples, feel them spring hard to his touch, because she is smart and funny and doesn't seem to know how much she knows—and her eyes, her tender yet piercing eyes. No question, their barter has been more than a fair trade. She needs guidance, nudges, and reassurance, as all artists do. He enjoys painting her, nude. There are fringe benefits to being an artist. He catches himself then, remembers Jane's fiancé due to pick her up at nine a.m., his no-longer passionate wife whom he still loves passionately, his desire to be faithful, the surely futile struggle to find here in rural Pennsylvania another model non-prudish enough to pose nude in barter for time and space and, he suspects, too sophisticated to be insulted or persuaded by his desires should he ever slip and attempt to indulge them. Rubbing the tip of his nose with the back of one hand, he reaches for the feathering brush with the other.

On her left hip, Jane's innocent fingers float ready to extend toward the easel, as though the thought has left her brain but not yet teased her fingers. Her legs, slightly parted at the groin, reveal a hint of dark feathered curls. Her smooth-boned knee rests on her muscled calf. Her toes, in full sun now, extend straight with the grace of a ballerina en pointe. With peripheral vision, she watches a white cat leap from loft to windowsill.

John steps back from his easel, the first panel of a planned triptych, smiles, and thinks, Patience is a virtue. With the Canon SLR digital camera, he takes several non-flash shots of Jane on the studio set to record the exact lighting. Then for no reason he can justify, he takes a photo of the current state of the painting on his easel but at an angle in order to include the real Jane, still posing. After he transfers all to the laptop via the thin white cable, he nods to Jane and motions the paintbrush toward her.

"Any questions, madame?" John asks.

Yes, Jane thinks, *Why is your manner sometimes so rude. It's not hard to say, Please clean the brush for me now.* But his manner comes with their barter, so she doesn't speak her mind and chalks up this quirk to his eccentric side. She rises, stretches, decides not to ask where he was born, throws on her jeans and V-neck burgundy sweater, slips on black moccasins. She has only an hour to paint before her fiancé arrives.

The paintbrush suddenly stops twitching in John's hand. He is gazing at the screen of the laptop—at the photo of Jane in the background, his painting of her in the foreground. With her index fingers and thumbs, Jane composes a frame of John at the laptop screen. "Wouldn't it be interesting, sir, to paint the image of you, the artist, viewing the computer screen that shows the image on your easel beside the original posed image of me, the model? Sort of a telephone-tag, multimedia scene of a scene of a scene? Like mirrors reflecting one another but with subtle distortions—no, not distortions but rather different perceptions—when one looks hard enough?"

John turns to stare at her, through her. "That's what I was thinking. You scare me, madame," he says.

"I'm sorry, sir," Jane says, although she has no idea for what she's apologizing.

"The answer depends on the astuteness of the viewer, the seer, I suppose," John says.

Jane doesn't understand. The answer? To what question? His mind fascinates her. She grasps the wood end of the brush and removes it gently from his fingers.

John grabs his car keys from the table to leave for his part-time day job. "My students need their sleep—at least my geometry lecture is good for something," he says.

"Surely you exaggerate," Jane replies. If he were her fiancé, she'd rub his back, tickle his ear.

"Would you die with me, madame?" John asks as he shuts the door behind him.

Stunned, Jane drops the brush, which bounces off both her new black moccasins before rolling to the floor—carnelian splotches everywhere. Looking at the door John just closed behind him, she wills the new open door to him in her mind to latch shut with as firm and resounding a click. The mental door won't budge. This is insanity. Why *does* he intrigue her so? Does *his* question wander in *her* mind, too, disguised by different words? Her curiosity burns, a danger signal she's come to know. She builds a wall then between herself and

John, a brick wall with peepholes in the mortar through which she may adore but no more, pledges herself to that boundary for now and always, never to cross, even though never is a very, very long time.

The familiar *honk-honk-honk* of her fiancé's car breaks Jane's rhythm. She steps back from the wet oils on her canvas, the first panel of a planned triptych, based on her pose for John. She smiles, finds her fingertips at her cheek. The horn honks longer, insistent. She drops the brush into a jar of muddy turpentine, which will annoy John—he wants the brushes dry when he arrives—but she doesn't have time to clean up properly. She grabs her purse, heads for the door, imagines her fiancé's surliness when he sees her paint-splotched shoes, goes back to clean and dry the brush for John, planning to say when her fiancé complains of her lateness, "Why, yes, I did have a good painting session, thanks for asking," and planting a kiss on his rugged cheek, ignoring his ill humor, placing her faith in this good Christian man who received her virginity with such stoic calm.

The Second Panel

My dear ally, your aura is flaming with brew!

—Pleoneveia, *Somniare Perferre Canere Saltare,* line 99

Afternoon sun, its summertide glare muted by an ochre silk panel, floods the studio through a remodeled, rolled-open, and fully screened ceiling. John, now a salt-and-pepper-haired artist in sandals, jeans, and rolled-up sleeves, brushes bold strokes of oil on a newly primed canvas. In front of a royal purple drape, Jane poses nude on the wide seat of a dark walnut Queen Anne chair. A white streak in her leonine mane frames the right side of her face. At the top of the chair, carved pineapples extend like rays from the sun. Her head leans into baroque swirls on the carved chairback, and her gaze is fixed on middle space between herself and John. The Third Movement of Beethoven's *Pastoral,* "Merry Assembly of Country Folk," swells from the DVD/CD player in the western corner.

"So what do you think of the European Union?" John asks with a hint of humor in his voice.

A new game of his, twenty years into their barter and friendship, asking her questions while she poses and cannot answer. She smiles in her head at his titter of laughter behind the easel. After his divorce, he had roamed Europe for half a year, painting and pondering. He permitted Jane full use of his studio in exchange for its maintenance. A healthy plan for her, the studio being the only familiar continuum spanning her divorce and move to a new apartment, which she grew to love once the night terrors of loneliness and fear ceased, once she started to dream of John's companionship and return so they could pick up where they left off, as though nothing had changed yet with everything changed—no spousal fidelities left to divide them. Hope flickers on dust motes in the air.

In the uncomfortable position imposed by John, Jane's body is tilted toward the right in the high-backed chair. Her right leg rests over the curved chair arm, her hand capping the knee. A touch of arthritis keeps her toes from pointing straight. With thighs spread wide and her left shin behind the cabriole chair leg, her painted purple toenails peek around the chair's ball-and-claw foot. Tarnished mirrors reflect muted sun into the one dark shadow of her body.

Jane grasps at the pose "zone," tries to sense John's sense of the scene, but his post-Europe senses seem prurient and foreign to her way of thinking. Why not just paint a Georgia O'Keeffe flower, she asked him last week, to which he responded in an exasperated patronizing manner that he "seeks the essence of creation in the flesh—the vagina open wide as double church doors on a Sunday morn." As if he'll find god up there. During her eventually celibate marriage, she cared for herself physically enough to learn that god was not up there—anatomy-wise, anyway. She passes off the change in John as something to do with the kinship of loss and lust, which she read about somewhere, and which she hopes is a passing phase—in her as well. A very present problem is the titillation of his touch as he poses her limbs to suit his visual whims. His lingering glance at her spread thighs when he positioned her left shin behind the cabriole chair leg. *Can I love you?* she thinks, wanting to trust again in trust. Under the easel, she sees John scratch a mosquito bite on his ankle with the tip of his brown leather sandal. A white cat leaps from loft to windowsill and, its tail twitching, laps milk from a saucer with a pink sandpaper tongue.

Scents of summer apple blossoms and freesia waft past the cat on humid breeze.

"So where have you hidden your new paintings?" John calls from behind the easel.

She laughs in her mind and suddenly recalls the brick wall she constructed there so long ago to maintain the professional boundary between herself and John. The wall fell into disuse in his absence, disintegrated into dust. She's always liked John, too much perhaps, but always controlled it before, never broke her vows. Had he figured somehow, though, in her divorce? Had she in his? No matter. They are both free now. John seems lonely, too, but randomly irritable—of course, he always was. Maybe he doesn't know yet what he wants. Maybe she doesn't either.

He seems in a good mood today, perhaps because he's drinking so much, been drinking too much since his return. Maybe it's a European custom he's adopted for good, Jane muses. She buries her worries and tries to meld her mind with his vision, this "essence of creation in the flesh," her vulva opened wide for posterity.

"Jane, are you thirsty?" John calls from behind the painting, wiping sweat from his brow and taking a sip of vodka on the rocks. The ice is melting fast in the heat.

No answer. He peers around the easel, sees her maintaining pose. Her left arm, straight up, exposes some cellulite puckers at the inner arm, bent at elbow, hand behind her neck and out of sight. A dew of perspiration on her brow seems serendipitous, and he decides to add it to the painting. Reaching for the pigment box without looking, he knocks a navel orange to the floor. He fishes in the box for iridescent white, rose dore, and terra verte to mix. The orange, midway between ripe and rot, rolls on oak planks to the eastern wall. Above it, pollinating bees hum and flick against the window screens, which bulge inward with profuse blooms of yellow cockscomb and Roman Roses.

"Tell me when," he calls.

When, she thinks.

She marvels at their ease together, the pleasure of their resumed companionship. Funny, she's been trying to help heal him after his divorce, and here he is healing her. After noting its exact position on her knee and the curvilinear arm of the Queen Anne chair, she reaches her right arm behind her neck and grasps from her left hand a little 50-mL bottle of vodka, without having to move her problematically posed left arm. She drains the entire little bottle.

She's drinking too much, too, but she doesn't want to appear stupid next to his now-more-global knowledge, and they both seem to like the wordplay and ideas for new paintings that spill unbidden from their lips when loosened by vod. She's gotten carried away in banter a few times after posing; so has he, but never more than in a glazed-eye allusive way. She looks forward to chatting after their session today, since he's begun to linger to watch her at work.

Through their talk and shared art over the years, she has seen a myriad synchronicities, some as simple as belief in signs. Now she wonders if, since his return, she has been hearing things she wants to hear, reading into things, seeing things that aren't there, not seeing things that are. *Could you love me?* If only she could ask, but she can't, and she feels aroused, *very* aroused. She breaks pose to look down. No tangible thing touches her down there. *Not again.* She yearns. She burns. She hears him turn behind the easel, shoves the empty bottle into her left hand, and snaps her right arm back to position. She must remember to buy bottled water on the way home.

John strides directly to her, taps the tip of a #3 shader brush against his graying beard, meets her gaze full on. She cannot move her eyes—must maintain pose. His nose is splotched with vermilion, the brilliant red pigment derived from cinnabar. She smiles inside her head; her desire sparks into flame.

"Jane, what *have* you done with your fingers?" John lifts her right hand in his, kisses her palm (she does not move), reposes it on her knee and the arm of the chair.

She feels it coming, cannot stop it, cannot help it, cannot stop it.

John returns to the easel and wonders why her nose is red. Maybe she's catching a summer cold. Good thing he's drinking vodka—just what the doctor ordered. He already knows he'll stay afterward today. He's enjoyed painting her for years, never thought until his return to enjoy watching *her* paint, her bold strokes, her patience with detail, her slow breathing, the way her fingers move with expression.

Cannot stop it, cannot help it. A black dog jumps to the outer windowsill and barks. Cannot allow it. Startled, the cat runs and hides under the throne. Cannot stop it. Cannot help it. Cannot—Must not. Her orgasm clutches, and she writhes, but it is different this time. It shudders up, ripples her solar plexus, arcs in blue sparks around her heart, and surges up to her mind, where it explodes and explodes and explodes and explodes, hidden behind the bone of her skull. Full circle.

John steps out from behind the easel, sees the flush from her nose now on her cheeks, on her chest, and knows something has happened. He ponders her name as he has done so many times before, but this time it is different: Jane Doe, a mysterious unknown woman who he increasingly wants to *know,* who somehow merges the long-haired girl with freckles who he played with next door as a child and the nude flushed woman pregnant with possibilities only eight feet away, with hard beckoning nipples. If only he could trust again, love again.

She breaks pose and turns her sloe eyes to meet his blue. Rippled space touches and tousles gray hair at his left earlobe, kisses his forehead, kisses him between the eyes, home of the third eye at least, kisses it again. Aroused, he steps back behind the easel, gets himself in check, but smears his hand on the painting through ochre and terra verte.

Disgusted, he's ready to call it quits for the day, but strange sounds distract at the window screens. Every few seconds a *flap, tap,* and *whoosh* sound of dropping, then a new, unfamiliar birdsong—exquisite, tender, longing—then a *flap, tap,* and *whoosh* drop, the longing call but with added syllables and different inflection, a *flap, tap,* and *whoosh.*

"What *is* that, madame?" John calls. No answer. *Flap, tap, whoosh,* and the creative bird song, which this time sounds like, "Could you love me?" Confused, he peers around the easel at Jane, who is maintaining the pose. He peers around the other side of the easel at the screened windows, ducks, stands on tiptoe, searches for movement in flowered bushes and shrubs.

Jane hears the birdsong, too, which sounds oddly like, "Will you die with me?" John must be having fun with her. She plays back: "Will you live with me?"

John hears the new refrain. Impossible. And yet? How many vods has he downed today? "Jane—we're done. Come help me look for that bird."

Walking slowly with measured steps, she joins him at the easel, curious, aware of her nakedness. "There it is," she says, pointing. "A female cardinal."

The cardinal rests on the branch of a swaying Rose of Sharon and suddenly flaps at the screen, taps it with her beak, and drops in a *whoosh* down to the outer sill.

"What is she doing?" Jane asks with alarm. The cardinal flits back to the Rose of Sharon, appears to stare through the screen as if she knows what she seeks, thrusts herself at it again, and falls.

"Maybe she thinks her chicks are in here?" John ventures, pointing to a ceramic statue of three chicks on the window ledge.

"Or her mate. Cardinals mate for life, you know. Could he possibly be in here, sir?" Jane asks, looking up for a splash of red wings or a gash in the screened ceiling.

"She'll break her neck," John says. "I think I should frighten her away, madame."

Jane nods and follows him slowly to the window. John places his hand on the screen and rubs it softly. "Fly away, my sweet, your mate's not here." The cardinal freezes for a second in the Rose of Sharon and disappears in a flash of rustling leaves.

"Yes he is," says Jane. John turns to look for red wings but sees only Jane's crimson lips, partly open in sheer wonder, only inches away. Their eyes meet. Doubt dissolves. Lips touch—hesitant, then tender, hungry, famished. As they sink to the floor, a foot knocks the orange, which rolls to the throne and the white cat underneath, which bats the orange, leaps to an urn, to the top of the canvas, and up to the loft, where she purrs along to decades-long-in-the-waiting lovemaking below.

Later, as they lie cradled in each other's arms, Jane wonders aloud whose lips sought whose first, and she marvels that they not only came together but whispered "My god" together, too, as if with the same voice from the very same throat. Outside, the black dog barks, barks again, races and growls after prey, which flaps and flutters and screams, and something is flung against the window screens. The female cardinal's head thuds at an odd angle, her neck droops into a U, she *whoosh*-drops from sight, and yellow-brown goo oozes down the screen.

Jane gasps and huddles into the fetal position. John doesn't know what to do, adores her but can't let them pursue this "love thing" now—he's not ready, and probably neither is she—runs his hand up her spine, rubs her hair, straddles and embraces her from above, offering her protection in the only way he knows how. This was a horrible mistake.

Jane half rises, face streaked with tears. "Why did she let herself get caught?" she asks.

John deliberates, chooses his words with care. "Because her mate isn't here," he says. He glances up at the ooze wending like thick honey down the screen.

Jane sees the miniscule ooze reflected in his pupils and eyes him quizzically. His face is tender but masked. His meaning slowly sinks in.

"No," she says, but her horror does not pierce his gravity. "You can't just—" She cups his cheeks in her hands. "I need you. We need each other. We have for years."

"Need is not enough. I'm not ready," he says, turning his back to her as he pulls on his jeans, zips.

"But I *am* ready, sir," Jane says, placing a hand on his freckled back.

"How can you be so sure?" John asks, reaching for his sandals. "We shouldn't have crossed this boundary, Jane. It will change everything."

"It already has," Jane whispers.

Weeping without sound, she watches him dress. Feels bubbles of anger boil deep within. Or is it heartbreak? She can't tell the difference. Why not? Does he feel the same confusion? He won't look at her. She thinks too late to wipe away tears so she can see clearly and memorize the pattern of freckles on his back. His shirt flutters over them. She removes her hand.

"I only ever wanted to be kind," John says, pulling his car keys from his jeans pocket.

"Me, too." Jane mouths the words to his back, no breath left to fuel her voice.

John steps back from the scene he just painted, the second panel of a planned triptych. He reaches for his fifth (sixth?) vodka, hears ice clink against glass, and thinks, Musicians strummed us too loudly that day, and There is life after hope's death, but I'm done with love because it's done with me, has shunned me from the beginning and always will, and She wouldn't wait, and now I want her too late. Damn women—their math never adds up. He sets the empty glass on the taboret, notices the dried ooze stuck to the screen, pokes it out with short stabs of the tip of an X-acto knife blade.

In her own studio now, Jane steps back from the scene she just painted, the second panel of a planned triptych. Her hand clutches a green mug of vodka to her heart. A nightingale sings in the distance. She peers up out the window at an M, the upside-down W of Cassiopeia, forever waiting in her chair, low in the sky. She thinks of Beatrice's line in *Much Ado About Nothing,* "They swore you were well-nigh dead for me." She throws the vodka through the screen and thinks, How mysterious God is—we cannot know how much we care until we care enough to let it go. She feels divine, sets the mug on the windowsill, and clasps her hands to restore humility, at which her throat constricts three times and clamps shut. She can't breathe and thinks, See the Man in Woman to see the human in both; or, no, is it, See the Woman in Man to see them both? Dizzy, she stumbles toward a mahogany rocking chair, feels loneliness and love implode in her chest, carnelian splotches everywhere, hidden behind the bone of her sternum.

The Third Panel

A DRAMA

> While the very air gasps and spews,
> Waves fling toward the sky, the void,
> As black as grottos, cold as limestone caves,
> That Elysium weeps.
>
> Swollen waves consume them.
> For days they plunge deeper.
> Their feet at last reach a molten sea floor.
>
> —Pleoneveia, *Somniare Perferre Canere Saltare,* lines 482-488

(Midnight. The whirlwind of Fall's frenzy, pungent with musty leaves and dislodged rot, floods darkly into an art studio's open wall-to-wall windows. From a lofty height, a sphere of blinding light illuminates below a bright circle of floor in which a black dog with peridot eyes stalks a braced white cat. Barely visible in shadow, a man and woman vie across the ring of light.

The first note of "Thunderstorm," *the* *Fourth Movement* *of Beethoven's* Pastoral, *crashes from above. The sphere spins, and many-mirrored facets glare glare on fair squares of bare bare skin: his forehead, his eye, his ear, her ear, her eye, her forehead. Autumn's maelstrom sucks them backward rather than down, an unnatural spatial ninety-degree shift. They strain against it in random thrusts toward each other and the light.)*

John: Will you die with me?

Jane: Yes, John, I will. I will die the little death with you as often as we wish, as long as we can, up until the good death. And after that. And after that as well, at Home.

John: I don't believe you, woman. Try again.

(Lightning streaks and thunder claps impair both their sight and hearing.)

Jane: What? Are you there?

(He doesn't answer but leans into the wind to move closer to the light.)

Jane *(flustered and trying to maintain control)*: You look glum, man. Why did you keep painting me?

John *(trying to maintain control)*: I am not dumb. Why did you keep posing for me?

(Reflected light lurches and mottles their bare shoulders.)

Jane: Why, indeed?

(Black Dog launches a vertical slow-motion leap. White Cat cowers.)

John: Will you die with me?

Jane: Sigh with you?

John: Die with me.

Jane: Try with you?

John: DIE WITH ME.

(Black Dog's paw bats a bullet of reflected brilliance into Jane's eyes.)

Jane: I can't see you. I've seen too much. Where are you? Who are you? What is death? I was just trying to be kind—you know, bear one another's burdens? I'm so sorry, please forgive me, I got drunk and carried away.

(Black Dog's paw kicks a bullet of reflected brilliance into John's ears.)

John: I can't hear you. I've heard too much. And who are *you* to help? I don't trust your motives. I'm so sorry, please forgive me, I got drunk and carried away. I was just trying to be kind. I can't take this anymore.

Jane: Make war? Why?

John: Ach du lieber.

(The whirlwind sucks John harder, and he recedes from Jane.)

Jane: Don't go. I'm having an existential CRISIS here.

John: I hear you, SEXUAL COERCIONIST.

Jane: Now there's a mouthful.

John: I can hear you, you know.

Jane: I see that, VOYEUR.

John: Cut the bawdy comedy.

Jane: What do you mean? Sexual coercionist is a lead-heavy six syllables. What did you think I meant? Are you drunk?

John: Seven syllables—are *you* drunk?

Jane: Five fingers of vod under my belt.

John: Mon Dieu. I can't help you. I'm having a rough time myself.

(The whirlwind sucks Jane harder, and she recedes from John. The faces of the mirrored sphere fuse into one and reveal John and Jane's wholly mottled bodies. They spy their nakedness; screams echo in the chamber like drunken pagan drums.)

Jane: I CAN'T die with you. I'm afraid.

John: What?

Jane: I'm AFRAID.

(Black dog drools in slow motion over their heads.)

John: AFRAID OF WHAT?

Jane: I am NOT fat.

John: I am NOT a cad.

Jane: I am NOT a twat—but I applaud you.

John: I do NOT have the clap. ADIEU.

Jane: NO.

John: I'm trying not to melt, madame. Run, Jane, RUN.

Jane: I'm melting, sir. Run, Dick, RUN.

John: I'm NOT a DICK.

Jane: I KNOW that. You're an ANGEL.

John: I never had an ANGLE. (Did I?) Did *you?*

Jane: How DARE you? You RAPIST.

(The blinding spotlight goes dark. Scenes of sexual abuse flash in the darkness around Jane.)

John *(shuddering)*: WHAT? I am NOT them.

(A mob of angry violent women emerge in the darkness around John.)

Jane: Don't you know me well enough by now to know I am NOT them?

(The maelstrom pounds with ear-numbing thunder.)

John: ADIEU.

Jane: WHAT DO YOU MEAN, "I DO?" WHAT IS HAPPENING, SIR?

John: MADAME, I CAN'T DO THIS NOW.

Jane: I WON'T GIVE UP ON US, SIR.

(The blinding spotlight resumes its brilliance. Their skulls part and fall, revealing secrets in gray matter. Shrieking, they cover their eyes with their hands. The whirlwind stops so abruptly they are flung forward past each other into cover of darkness across the ring, to where the other had just stood. Each peeks back through parted fingers, and the whirlwind starts anew, sucking them farther from the spotlight, where Black Dog's drool pools. White Cat leaps from sight, but the fixed scale of her tail fails and stays in the light. Black Dog lands in a triumphant crouch and grows, eyes aglow. The wall-to-wall windows shear, buckle, and shatter under a tidal flood of sea, trees, rainfall, and mud. The flood sucks Jane and John down into murky liquid smoke. The blinding light explodes. Sapphire and peridot orbs probe the darkness.)

REFLECTIONS ON THE DRAMA

His

> He pondered his losses, and anguish clung.
> Then he recalled her grace, her faith
> In God, on whom she depended
> For well-being and sustenance.
>
> ... And so the Lord
> Nudges those who seek help
> From everyone else.
>
> —Pleoneveia, *Somniare Perferre Canere Saltare,*
> lines 512-515, 518-520

Alone in his studio, John steps back from the scene he just painted, a maelstrom, the third panel of a planned triptych, and thinks, Third time's sure not the charm this time. This damn panel is hopeless. Like his behavior in the supermarket the other day, when he spotted Jane at the fresh produce section—she loved avocados and greens—and he spun the cart on its wheels in the opposite direction so she wouldn't see him.

Get a grip, man. Someone had to have the courage, prudence, and self-control to build a dam: "This far you may come, and no farther"—Job 38:11. Why does that sound so heartless, so unjust? And yet, self-love must be greater than selfless love, because we cannot truly help anyone else unless we love ourselves first. Hardly a new thought—according to Aristotle, "a good person must be a self-lover, because he will help himself as well as others by performing fine actions." I only hope it will help Jane that I built a dam. I guess we cannot know how much we care until we kiss kindness goodbye. That sounds logical. I should be the epitome of calm.

But I feel far from calm. Either I'm *missing* something, or *something* is missing. Maybe that's it—something is missing. In me? Or in the triptych—a missing panel? A panel about what? What do I want viewers of the panel to see, feel, think? What do *I* want to see, feel, think? The art's sending me on wild goose chases. What does math tell me? There's no equation for hope. At least not yet. Maybe an interdisciplinary study: geometry —> the fourth dimension —> the fifth dimension —> the fifth element —> the fourth or fifth something. Good god, this could take years. I'd much rather paint.

Something lands on top of John's head. He flinches down and looks up, sees no spider web strands, and sighs with relief yet reaches hesitant fingers to his hair. A feather? A white feather. His mouth drops agape. So much more to learn on this road to self-discovery. Think Hope, man.

He turns to his laptop, doesn't know where to begin his research. Come on, think outside the box, brainstorm, even if the method seems ludicrous. The letter "f" seems important. Feather. Fractured fractals? Or more likely "four" or "five" or "fifth." He flinches as though goosed. Through the door in his mind still open to Jane, a new door beckons.

Hers

> Stripped of her faith, she cries from the stone:
> "Joy has fled. Grief overwhelms,
> Smothers my soul. Love has flown. My sole trust,
> Mentor, and ally—lost? dead?" ...
>
> "Before my hope always sustained, pure and true." ...
>
> "To whom do I pray now for miracles of rescue?"
>
> —Pleoneveia, *Somniare Perferre Canere Saltare,*
> lines 600-603, 609, 615

Alone in her studio, Jane steps back from the scene she just painted, a whirlwind, the third panel of a planned triptych, throws her brush to the floor, and thinks, This panel is just wrong wrong wrong. Like her behavior in the supermarket the other day, when she spotted John at the fresh fish section—he loved Pacific Chinook salmon—and she turned her cart and fled; it hurt too much to see him.

I'm boxed in. The panel is boxed in—leaves no room for growth, for hope, for what I want to express. What *do* I want to express? John's kindness kills me softly with paint. My kindness kills him loudly with paint. Kindness can kill as a two-edged sword. We cannot know how much we care until we kiss kindness goodbye.

But, What *is* kindness, really? Is it a byproduct of the evolution between self-love and selfless love? And what of their definitions? Could self-love be Aristotle's definition, which I learned from John? Could selfless love be C. S. Lewis' definition—a love that is passionately committed to the well-being of the other? Kindness may well vary with the level at which each person is evolving. And the goal may *not* be pure selfless love at all but rather a meeting with self-love halfway—say, at 5 on a scale of 0 to 10. Is the meridian between self-love and selfless love the home of kindness?

As though playing scales on a piano, she counts aloud with the fingers of her left hand, left to right:

0, 1, 2, 3, 4

She counts aloud with the fingers of her right hand, right to left:

10, 9, 8, 7, 6

Her mouth drops agape. There *is* no 5. It falls somewhere between my hands. She touches her forearms. There must be something to this—I'm getting goose bumps.

Damn, someone has to build an image of hope. What does one look like? Think HOPE, Jane. Open up, brainstorm. Maybe a multidisciplinary approach? Five disciplines. Geometry, vanishing points, perspectives, knaves in naves. That's four, and they're not all unrelated. Chances in chancels? That's just wordplay, not real. Good God, this could take years.

She climbs to the loft, her library and study, turns on her laptop, Googles "nave," reads the record-holders on Wikipedia, and copies and pastes into a notes document: "Longest nave in Denmark: Aarhus Cathedral, 93 metres (305 ft). Longest nave in Ireland: St Patrick's Cathedral, Dublin, 91 metres (299 ft) (externally). Longest nave in Italy: St Peter's Basilica in Rome, 91 metres (299 ft), in four bays."

Where's my Bible? Where's my art book on cathedrals? That's it: *cathedrals.* Through the door in her mind still open to John, a new door beckons.

The Fourth Panel

Day shall follow brightly
The doubts, the dark.
Hope will not forsake those
Who struggle through strife with wavering faith,
Who ultimately trust all shall be well
With all of their power and risen belief.

—Pleoneveia, *Somniare Perferre Canere Saltare*, lines 696-701

HER WAY

Life Gets in the Way

Jane knows full well the extent to which she'd become overwhelmed, organizationally speaking, with the concept of a fourth image for her planned triptych. No triptych by definition includes a fourth image, but intuition tells her that the whirlwind in the third panel is crucial AND that the triptych is meaningless, or at least not resolved, without a cathedral interior. Not knowing yet whether she'll scrap one of the panels or assemble a quadriptych, she forges ahead with a painting of a cathedral interior. The result is lacking, and disappointment gnaws as viscerally as hunger. For proper inspiration, she realizes, she *must* listen while painting to the First Movement of Beethoven's *Pastoral*, "Awakening of Cheerful Feelings on Arriving in the Country."

Before she can begin a second attempt at the image, she lands a job as an artist in the creative department of a second-rate, understaffed ad agency that eats up far more than a 9-to-5 and even some weekends and holidays. Most of her male co-workers are too young and neither interest nor attract her, and she avoids involvements, even friendships with women her age. She hates her self-imposed loneliness as well as the concept and stress of producing on demand, but the job calls for art production—no small thing these days—and most importantly, it pays the bills. Uncomfortable with the hard-sell lack of subtlety in her young colleagues' ads, she lets intuition guide her in combining wordplay and visual play. She immerses herself in the work. Soon she consistently produces cleverly intuitive commercial questions in her artistic ads as well as, to her surprise, varying styles for the answers.

Two years into the job, past the initial challenge and miles beyond bored, she misses the leisurely intellectual searching for questions she can no longer remember from her pre-ad-world days. One evening, she sets her iPhone's alarm clock to arise at 4 a.m. to paint "her" way, not the ad-world way, except she isn't sure what her way is anymore, if she ever even had a personal style to begin with. John had said she did.

At the appointed time, doubt allows her little time to paint before the alarm rings again, this time calling her to paying work. Undaunted, she follows her plan with determination, returning each dawn to the same cathedral interior view she had painted two years earlier—how can time pass so quickly?—but this version in a baroque style with an ornate interior. It's a good painting but still lacking—something, but what?

She wishes she could ask John, whose wisdom and mentorship she recalls at stymied junctures like this. She still thinks of him at bedtime, too, or in the wee hours, though far less often than when they'd parted, which seems a lifetime ago. She wonders idly what he is doing now, how he is, remembers with fondness his company and conversation, the touch of his hand, but she forces herself to relegate him, the person, to the past. Time to approach this artistic dilemma his way, though, mathematically, logically, yet intertwined with her innate belief in and awe of spirituality.

Jane's Research

In 1908, the United States Naval Academy Chapel was dedicated in Annapolis, Maryland. It underwent remodeling in 1940 to form the shape of a cross and increase available seating to 2,500 people. In 1961, the chapel was designated a national historic landmark, and it now holds both Catholic and Protestant services.

The chapel's many striking features include its bronze-paneled front door, interior arches, a 268-rank organ controlled by a 522-drawknob console, Tiffany stained-glass windows, and the breathtaking copper chapel dome, which rises 200 feet from the altar. The central portion of the dome consists of four concentric spheres. No lines cross the perfect orb of the first, innermost, sphere. Eight chords connect the first and outer spheres, creating eight triangles. Eight rays bisect the triangles and connect the second sphere to the outer sphere, creating sixteen arcs at the outer rim. Thirty-six star-like lights line the outer sphere. Beyond the outer sphere and down the curve of the dome, rays extend to meet the sides of arched windows at the base of the dome. Around the "sun" of the crucial central orb and its surrounding concentric spheres, the "sky" of the rayed dome contains 120 star-like lights.

Jane speculates that a viewer could perceive the windows at the base of the dome as logically positioned to allow sunlight into the cathedral. She wonders, though, if the central orb could be perceived as a skylight that allows Divine light to pass through the lenses of the surrounding spheres, past the starry field, through the clear glass windows at the base of the dome, and out into the world.

The Result

In her studio, Jane studies her huge pointillist oil painting, which she has named Queensbridge Cathedral. The church exists only in her mind but is so real to her that she has located it precisely three kilometers from the Giant's Causeway, County Antrim, Northern Ireland. She doesn't know why.

The cathedral's interior is massive in scale and in true perspective. The frontal view is from the nave and low—at the eye level of a white cat. The cat is lying on a lapis-blue carpet of a wide main aisle between dark pews that draw nearer to each other in the distance, where they stop before the altar, which is crowned with a cross. Behind the altar rises a tall stained glass window, which, near the vanishing point of the perspective, appears abstract to viewers, who assume they cannot ascertain the window's subject due to the "distance" between it and them. The window is flanked by two white pillars and capped by an arch crowned by ten white rays on a field of rippled gray.

A second tier of seating is visible through lapis-blue railings. Above the railings are large metal sconces and arched stained-glass windows, the repetition of which draws viewers' eyes forward to the inner sanctum of the dome above the altar. The dome is only partially visible, revealing side-by-side arched windows capped with rounded V's, upside-down and pointing up to what looks like a starry field that continues upward, but the main arch of the cathedral ceiling blocks further view. The main arch and walls bear the thematic palette of white and cerebral gray. The palette is less rose-warm than the area behind the altar and provides a serene counterpoint to the primarily lapis-blue spiritual theme of the scene, all of which draw focus to the altar at the base of the dome.

Reflections

Although the pointillist version holds promise, Jane moves on to a surrealist version of Queensbridge Cathedral with rays of sun through the many windows. She can perceive the rays as only softly prickly, which makes no sense. Next she paints the cathedral in what proves to be a dissatisfying and unfocused American Gothic style without the cat—a huge mistake because the cat now seems integral.

The following Sunday, she assesses all of her fourth-panel versions. Not one of them captures what she thinks she saw in her mind's eye five years ago, and she wonders if she'd decided on the wrong image in the first place. At which point her vision and skills seem irrelevant, her life seems irrelevant, she has no idea even what questions she should be asking, and she sinks into a pit of self-disgust, which festers to the extent she can't stand seeing the many canvases displaying her failed attempts, failed vision, failed skills, failed life.

She stacks the paintings in a rusted rack in the dusty back room of her studio, where she can never stop sneezing. As she tosses a paint-encrusted tarp over the rack, she sneezes for the fifth time, her eyes squeezed half shut, and she sees something in the painting on the end, something in the space between the dots in the pointillist version that she had not seen before, but her brain can't make sense of what her eyes see.

She removes the canvas from the end of the rack and carries it to the sunny window in the main studio room, where she studies it critically from several angles—close up, then from a distance. With her eyes squeezed half shut, she finally perceives, with great difficulty counting, a sixteen-spoked wheel. The only sixteen-spoked wheels she's ever seen are on a river paddleboat. John once told her, "It all begins with the river," which she never quite understood in or out of context, but she now feels an intuitive clarity that seems to transcend her painting and describe what's wrong in her life, maybe in many lives.

In her excitement, Jane ponders aloud, "Wheel = We'll. I must see the light before I can see the man—I mean art, spirituality, life."

The clarity is quickly spoiled by a sense of interminable effort thwarted by insufficient time—life, after all, is finite. How hard and long must she work to accomplish such clarity on canvas, and if she's lucky, in her life? On second thought, she's already fallen head over heels down a slippery slope and hit rock bottom. There is only one way out: up.

She steps back farther from the pointillist panel and closes one eye.

"*Sotto in sù?* What if I stand at the altar and look up at the dome from below?"

She contorts her body to see that view, which is clearly impossible because the cathedral dome proper is not visible in the painting, as any viewer of the scene would know.

"The dome looks like a silver skull spider, a granddaddy-long-legs, its disproportionately small body a diamond, with sixteen, not eight, legs splayed away from each other and spanning a sink in which a white cat sleeps. Did I actually paint a flat ceiling trompe l'oeil? Wait, I did paint flat, but not as a fresco, not as an intended illusion, and not on a ceiling. I painted it in oil on canvas, and my god, it's from the wrong perspective."

She brushes a minuscule speck off the canvas.

"Five *years* down the drain. Back to the drawing board."

Jane is baffled by her lack of self-disgust and in its place an exhilarating tingle of hope and an even more amazing and undeniable desire to share the hope with John. Without him, she finally realizes, she cannot be complete. Maybe now she can do it right with him, if he is amenable to the idea.

White Cat *(alone on stage)*: |Spirituality| + |Free will| + Providence = Predestination.

HIS WAY

Life Got in the Way

John's third panel irritates him more each time he looks at it because the maelstrom is too dark, too hopeless, and just plain wrong as the last panel of a triptych, which had begun with such promise. And the fourth panel, his myriad versions of it—every conceivable artistic rendering of the letter "f" and the number "5"—infuriate him because no logical transition exists between the third and fourth panels as they stand. In fact, his time-consuming exploration of artistic styling for "f" and "5" now strikes him as daft. The blame lies with him—he'd given himself permission to pursue ludicrous methods.

For peace and inspiration, he plays the First Movement of Beethoven's *Pastoral*, "Awakening of Cheerful Feelings on

Arriving in the Country." Once the music relaxes him, he finds himself thinking of Jane after all these years, of soliciting her feedback, which had usually proven helpful, even if only to encourage him to envision his subject in a different light, from a different perspective, or on a broader scale.

Searching back through memory, he can't recall his rationale for running away to Europe after his divorce, when he could have turned to Jane for solace and understanding. And then, once back and working again with Jane, running away from her, too, after their ill-timed lovemaking. Perhaps *it* wasn't ill-timed. Perhaps *he* was ill-timed, not ready. That's it. Not ready. And he'd considered her not ready as well.

Perhaps he'd been as wrong in those deductions as in these blasted third and fourth panels. Time to approach this artistic dilemma her way, spiritually, yet intertwined with his innate beliefs: mathematics, logic, and academic study resulting in a well-informed plan. Strange he is an artist given those beliefs, yet he is who he is, someone gifted with equal predominance of both hemispheres of his brain. High time to use them together as he used to do with Jane, who complemented him in a way no other woman could.

John's Research

I

Fillipo Brunelleschi (1377-1446), born in Florence, Italy, was perhaps the greatest architect and engineer of the early Renaissance. His studies centered on literature and mathematics. During 1402-1404, he visited Rome's ancient monuments, noting in particular the Pantheon dome, and studied the De

Architectura manuscript, the only extant work of Marcus Vitruvius Pollio (circa 75-15 BC), a Roman architect, engineer, and writer. Brunelleschi was the first known artist (circa 1425) to paint in geometric and optical linear perspective, which depicted two-dimensional objects in three dimensions as a mirror would reveal them; his innovation advanced the art of painting throughout the Renaissance.

Brunelleschi designed the Santa Maria degli Angeli in Florence, an oratory for a monastery. Building began in 1434, rose to fifteen feet, stopped in 1437 due to lack of funds, and was not completed until the 1930s. An aerial view reveals the octagonal dome and the sixteen-sided exterior, which John intuits as significant. He can't explain why—neither the significance of eight or sixteen nor his reliance on intuition.

Brunelleschi is best known for designing Il Duomo on the Basilica di Santa Maria del Fiore, a magnificent spectacle on the skyscape of Florence. Building of the cathedral proper began in 1296, the dome was completed in 1436, the façade was finished in the 19th century, and preservation of Il Duomo is ongoing. The cathedral forms a large cross. By law, in Brunelleschi's time, the dome could not be supported by exterior buttresses, so he invented a new form of architecture for the Dome. With the Roman formula for concrete lost in time, he designed the Dome of four million bricks and mortar to sit above the cathedral roof on a drum, or windowed octagonal lantern, to allow heavenly light to flood the Dome. The innovative design required more inventions, and Brunelleschi devised construction machinery and tools such as hoisting machines and the lewis, derived from the Latin *leuis* meaning "to levitate," which enabled the raising of large stones. John speculates that an astute and spiritual viewer of the self-supporting Dome could well imagine it supported by angels, not by ingenious and innovative engineering.

Many paintings adorn the inside of the basilica, such as Domenico di Michelino's *Dante and the Divine Comedy* (1465). John loves the artistic joke in this painting, which among scenes from the *Divine Comedy* depicts Dante in a 1465 view of Florence, which he could not have seen in his lifetime (1265-1321).

II

> I saw the angel in the marble and carved until I set him free.
>
> The greater danger for most of us lies not in setting our aim too high and falling short, but in setting our aim too low and achieving our mark.
>
> —Michelangelo

Michelangelo Buonarroti (1475-1564) was an Italian painter, sculptor, architect, poet, and engineer. His brightly colored fresco of over 300 biblical scenes adorns the vaulted ceiling of Rome's Sistine Chapel, the most famous chapel in Vatican City. A new kind of scaffolding was created to rise from the floor instead of hanging from the ceiling, because suspended scaffolding would mar the dome surface and make it unusable for fresco painting. Near the highest tier of scenes, 68 feet from the floor, *The Creation of Adam* reveals God about to bestow life on the first man, whose sight and consciousness are raised at God's presence but whose finger floats in space, unaware of the imminent, life-giving touch of his Father's finger.

John first focuses on their index fingers. Next he gazes at where each one points. Then, with effort, he embraces both perspectives. A viewer could become mesmerized, John speculates, by the miniscule space between their fingers, even take out binoculars to study the space magnified. Of course, binoculars can zoom only so far into that mystery. Imagine the ability to travel infinitely into that space.

III

> I conceived, developed, and applied in many areas a new geometry of nature, which finds order in chaotic shapes and processes. ... Today you might say that, until fractal geometry became organized, my life had followed a fractal orbit.
>
> Clouds are not spheres, mountains are not cones, coastlines are not circles, and bark is not smooth, nor does lightning travel in a straight line.
>
> —Benoit B. Mandelbrot

Benoit B. Mandelbrot (1924-2010) was a Polish-born, French-American mathematician and the inventor of fractal geometry, in which an expression is repeatedly plotted and visualized as an iteration. The application has become a popular art form for its aesthetics, but academics and scientists value it more as a tool for analysis of phenomena in other fields, such as biological, physical, and social studies. John marvels that Mandelbrot—who studied under a tutor, mastered chess and maps, and became a fast reader—claimed to have never learned the entire alphabet.

In fractal geometry, $z_{n+1} = z_n^2 + c$ is the formula for the bounded iteration of the Mandelbrot set, a set of points in the complex plane, where phi (ϕ) is the argument of z in the z-plane, which symbolizes geometrically the complex numbers determined by a real axis and an imaginary axis at 90°. The equation creates a geometrical structure of figuratively unending space. John is fascinated by a visualized fractal of the Mandelbrot set, in which an image constantly recurs: a Buddha-like figure inclined 90°.

IV

> ...one cannot possibly understand mankind if one doesn't see that mathematics and poetry both have the same roots.
>
> So let us then try to climb the mountain, not by stepping on what is below us, but [by pulling ourselves up toward] what is above us, for my part at the stars; amen.
>
> —Maurits C. Escher

Maurits C. Escher (1898-1972) was a Dutch artist best known for his illusionist art, such as an artist's hands sketching themselves. He was also a poet and essayist. Although Escher was interested from an early age in music and carpentry, he failed most of his exams so never officially graduated. In his most famous art, Escher used perspective and precise understanding of non-Euclidian (geometric) space, as well as architectural principles, to create the illusion of impossible spaces. A viewer of Escher's illusionist art can see fixed and spatially impossible three-dimensional structures in two dimensions, where negative space transforms into a positive image, as when zooming into a fractal.

V

John is consumed by his question: If Brunelleschi's geometric and optical linear perspective, the mathematical model of Escher's art, and Mandelbrot's fractals can allow contemplation of the miniscule space between Adam and God's fingers, as Michelangelo depicted it on the ceiling of the Sistine Chapel, what might a viewer see, what might *I* see, while roaming its beauty?

Preparatory to trying to answer the question with paint, John follows his gut and researches further by writing a visual script for a soundless digital video exploring a cathedral interior. The script helps him establish the foundation and setting while focusing on the dome above, viewed from below, *sotto in sù.*

The Result

Fade in. The eye of the camera pans the round cathedral a full 360°. Columns with meandering marble veins stand erect, parallel, and equidistant. Stained-glass windows blaze with sunlit color. Marble statues pose as incense burns. The camera pans down and zooms out to capture the mosaic tile floor, a large sphere of four quadrants each bisected with rays, all stopping at a central concentric eye.

The camera pans up, seemingly contemplates the dome, and zooms in on the central wheel with its equally spaced waterfalls, shimmering silver against the sky-blue dome. In defiance of gravity, the silver waterfalls flow up and stop abruptly at the brilliant light in the middle eye of the wheel. As if to answer the questions, "Where does the silver water go? Where does it begin?", the camera pans down the waterfalls that divide the wheel into sixteen sections, and CGI permits a full cross section:

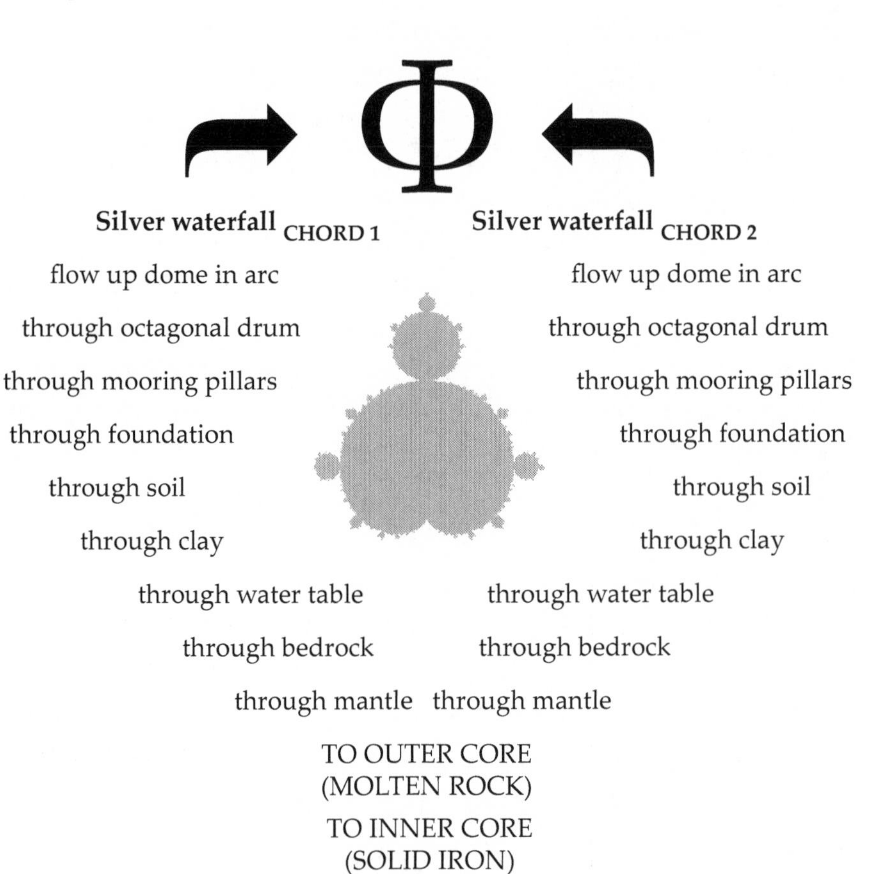

Plunge down one side; swim up the other. Full circle, except for the brilliant mysterious light in the middle of the dome, from which the silver waterfalls, now translucent, radiate out, forming eight sky-blue triangles labeled in small tiles at the outer rim. The camera zooms in on each label—

unintelligible language, but clearly with different symbols on each arc. The camera pans out to the eight triangles, four of which—at alternate vertical angles, opposite each other—contain a gem. Pearl faces onyx, and sapphire faces peridot. Currents buffet the gems in the silver water, and they twist and turn as if anchored from below.

Startling the viewer, the wheel starts to rotate. The tide of silver water turns 180° and falls. The intent viewer, trying to keep the gems in proper perspective, must circle with the wheel and may grow dizzy and fall. The pearl suddenly evolves into Jane. The onyx, John. The peridot, Black Dog. The sapphire, White Cat. Now transparent, the silver water tugs them backward. White Cat meows. Black Dog barks. Jane and John, dappled by light through silver water, arouse from wakeful sleeping. All drink the silver water and float to the surface, aligned. All thrust up against the tide toward the light, but not as one. Black Dog falters in his doggy paddle, strains to keep his nose above water, tongue lolling out. Jane, John, and White Cat sip again from the water and spit streams toward Black Dog's mouth. Fifteen streams of spat silver water land on Black Dog's tongue. No one else is visible. From where did the other streams originate? Black Dog swallows the spat water and revives, catches up with those he can see. Now, in true equilibrium, they thrust up and UP and UP and UP to unite in a sacred conclave, a heavenly grotto.

They see with like mind orange fingers of flame, the immense fire far below. Intuitively now, they incline 90° and rejoice at what they see, all on the same plane, so well lit. Lit by what? They look up, are blinded by empyrean light, and finally *C Y*.

Reflections

John knows full well how hypomanic he has become in his research to paint a usable fourth panel, which he has roughed out in charcoal. Determined to fight his way through the craziness to the other side—plunge down one side; swim up the other—he immerses himself in the resolution of the panel, draws conclusions, questions anew.

Her + me = Hermes. I must receive the light before I can receive the woman—I mean subject, artistic expression, life. I knew chemistry figured in the equation. Mercury: a silver-colored element, the only metal that at room temperature is liquid—between solid (body) and gas (spirit)—such that its components can move freely, so dense that an ingot of gold would float in it, and which when split by outside forces forms round globules that will readily unite. But is this right chemistry or wrong?

John reconsiders the cathedral dome he envisioned for his video script. The dome looks like a silver octopus, its body a diamond disproportionately small when compared to its sixteen, not eight, tentacles, which span a commode in which a miniature black dog is trapped. The octopus' tentacles curve away from each other and grow ever smaller toward the edge of the commode, effectively creating a non-Euclidian vanishing point and infinite space between hub and rim. I hadn't planned to paint in hyperbolic space, John realizes, but rather toward a dam in real space—or, rather, on canvas. Wait, I didn't paint an octopus at all, and, my God, it's from the wrong perspective.

He brushes a minuscule speck off the canvas. Five damn *years* down the toilet. Back to square one. Filled with disgust, he shoves the painting and easel backward to the floor. At the crash and splintering of wood, an unexpected tingle of hope surges through him and an even more amazing, undeniable desire to share it with Jane. Maybe he could get it right this time, or at least better, never abandon her again, if she is agreeable to such an idea.

Black Dog *(alone on stage)*: Free will + light + fluid dynamics + centrifugal force + centripetal force = the law of attraction.

LOOKING UP FROM BELOW: A DRAMA

(Curtain opens. Jane and John stand below the proscenium arch, stage right and stage left, respectively, where they remain throughout the Act. Their bodies are angled to face middle space, a center point in the audience. Initially, they address each other through the audience. Later, they address each other directly but do not look at each other. They look at each other only toward the end of the Act.)

Jane: Is the fresco on the domed ceiling a formula for harmony and coexistence?

John: Like a Miss Universe contestant, with heaving breasts, stating breathily into a microphone, "I dream every night for world peace"?

Jane: I can hear him. This is serious—please tell him to cut the comedy.

John *(bowing to audience)*: My apologies.

Jane: Is the fresco on the domed ceiling a mandala of the gate between the conscious and unconscious worlds? A yantra for meditative ritual? A Native American medicine wheel? A Wiccan wheel of the year? A Celtic cross? A halo? Is it a picture of a pure land made in prayer on paper tucked into a crack in the Western Wall, … a complex icon on the door of a mosque, … a rosary? Could the fresco on the domed ceiling represent all of these things?

John: Is it a baby's first sight of Mother? Or is it an aureola surrounding the whole blinding being of the Divine? Could it be the aureola of a nipple crusted with cancer, or of a nursing breast, spurting milk, in want of a baby to suckle?

Jane: Please ask him, What is it with all this breast talk?

John: I can hear her. This is serious—please tell her to cut the comedy.

Jane *(curtsying to audience)*: My apologies.

John: Is it a primer on higher consciousness that could prevent religious, or any, war but without an explication de texte?

Jane: Expli- what? Does he mean a thorough scrutiny and interpretation of a written text, often word by word?

John: Please thank her most kindly for the clarification.

Jane: Or is it an abecedary?

John: Does she mean an ABCs for a novice?

Jane: Please thank him for explicating my language.

John: Is it a path to higher consciousness through the third eye, which lives on the meridian between left and right hemispheres of the brain, or is it merely the cerebrospinal nervous system reawakening and—

Jane: —connecting the pituitary body, the size of a pea, and the pineal gland, the size of a tiny pine cone?

John: She took the words right out of my mouth.

Jane: Is it a mandala of human completion?

John: Is it an ethereal tube that permits microscopic

as well as telescopic vision? As in free movement within a fractal?

Jane: Is the fresco on the cathedral dome merely an illusion, a crazy vision of a whirling dervish, the painted ramblings of a lunatic?

John: There are plenty of lunatics around. Are you in the market for one?

Jane: Might it be a map of identity and self, no longer dammed by a diaphragm and skull?

John: Damn, I wanted that line.

Jane: Perhaps it is a model of the self. Maybe after God and my parents created my being, after life fractured it, and after family and friends buttressed it, only I can sculpt myself, through limited vision as I try to view)myself(through the lenses of my eyes as they search for the providence born before my birth. If anyone helps in the sculpting along the way, it is a gift from a true friend.

John: Many people no longer see God in their lives. Please ask her, What about them?

Jane *(shaping quote marks with her fingers around quoted words)*: I haven't "seen" God in years. The last time was long ago, five years after I started meditating, when I "saw" a white world. There, in an unending void of pure white sat my spirit, my inner child—a beautiful, innocent little girl with white hair, soft as feather down. The child sat beside a perfect white lion, and both the lion and the child smiled at me. They spoke no words yet welcomed me. The horrors of the world replayed on the girl's April-blue eyes, yet she smiled and smiled and leaned into and hugged the perfect white lion, who was at least five times her size. She buried her fingers in his mane and gently finger-combed the strands. She would stop occasionally to lean her head on his side, place her sensitive fingertips there to vibrate with his rumbling purrs because she could not hear them—there was no sound in that white world. I didn't want to leave, but my time there was over before I knew it, and I never saw the little girl and lion again. After that, I could "see" only black. Once, when searching for God in the starry void on the back of my eyelids, I saw an invisible index finger write soft letters patiently in the color of the spirit, lapis-lazuli blue: *I AM HERE.* I hold onto that as best I can.

John: You should paint that.

Jane: I think I just did.

John: Did you say we can sculpt ourselves as we would like to hear ourselves, and so on?

Jane: See—hear—imagine. Tomayto, tomahto. I guess I should stop looking for God in all the wrong places. That sounds familiar. Is that a line from a movie?

John: No, it's a line from a song. The song title is "Lookin' for Love," by Waylon Jennings, and the line is "looking for *love* in all the wrong places."

Jane: Does that mean I am searching for a man I can love with all of my being in order to find God again? Or am I looking for God to find the right man to love?

John: It all depends on your perspective.

Jane: I have a penchant for choosing the wrong perspective. *(She shudders. She shudders again.)* Oh, my god. I think I finally get it. Ding. And I think I get that, too. Ding. And that. Ding. Ding. Ding. *(She repeats a robotic motion with each utterance of "ding.")*

John: JANE. *(He snaps his fingers, and Jane freezes into a motionless silence.)* Your needle is stuck—you're skipping.

(Jane starts skipping in a circle like a little girl.)

John: Not that kind of skipping. Cut the comedy.

Jane *(returning to her original mark on the stage)*: It's not comedy—it's the way my brain works. John, I don't remember what you look like. *(Jane looks up at the top of the theater.)* Maybe the dome is a painting of I John 4:19: We love because God loved us first. ... I guess I'll never know ... or will eye?

John: Maybe it's a painting of I John 4:21: Those who love God must love their brothers and sisters, too. Which includes parents, children, partners, friends, neighbors, strangers, the global village. ... I guess I'll never know ... or wheel I ...?

Jane: Maybe it's a painting of Galatians 5:22-23: The fruit of the Spirit is love, joy, peace, patience, kindness, generosity, faithfulness, gentleness, and self-control. There is—

John: —no law against such things.

Jane: That sounds so right, but the list lacks forgiveness—none of us is perfect.

John: Maybe it's implied in that scripture, where the virtues intersect.

Jane: What a beautiful thought, from a brilliant mind. ... Now, my brain hurts from all this thinking. I'd really like just one finger of vodka.

John: Paging Dr. Smirnoff or Dr. Stoli! Is there a Dr. Smirnoff or Dr. Stoli in the house? *(He scans the audience and winks.)* Jane, blink once hard, open your eyes wide, and then relax.

(Jane complies.)

Jane: Can people relive the days of the Fall—try to do them over right?

(Two signs descend near Jane, but she cannot see them. The one lower and to the rear reads: Live/Right. The one over her head reads: Day/Daze.)

John: It wasn't all wrong, Jane, but regaining days is an illusion. What we can do is paint hope on the canvas of life.

Jane: If regaining days is an illusion, maybe the Fall is, too. Hypothetically speaking, why can't we just skip the Fall entirely? For the sake of knowledge, though, I would like to understand, Where did it all "go south"?

John *(blushing)*: Where do you think it "went south"?

Jane *(blushing)*: It had something to do with apples, I think, or nipples or vodka.

John: Maybe. Maybe not.

Jane: Am I supposed to know by osmosis what that means? *(rhetorical question)* Maybe St. Thomas Aquinas was right all along.

John: How so?

Jane: "Love takes up where knowledge leaves off."

Jane and John *(in unison)*: More questions may be posed, and there is no one answer. Each answer lives in the eye of the beholder.

(Jane kneels facing the audience, bows, clasps her hands for a count of two, and rises. John kneels facing the audience, bows, clasps his hands for a count of two, and rises. They turn and see each other.)

John *(smiling joyfully)*: Hi, Jane. I never expected to see you in the flesh after all these years. What's up, my dear?

Jane *(smiling joyfully)*: EVERYTHING.

John: Are you sure? Are we kinsmen?

Jane: Did I hear you correctly—kinswomen?

John: I see your point.

Jane: Shall we create a kinship? Create new words for a righting kinship? *(Two signs descend near John, but he cannot see them. The one lower and to the rear reads: Live/Write. The one over his head reads: Knight/Nights.)* For example, a fish's home is water. A flame, whose home is the sky, also needs water—without it, she would consume all around her and then herself as well. It is a fragile balance, because the fish does not want his water to extinguish her flame, and the flame does not want to fry the fish when he leaps for sheer joy. And yet, I wonder—if the flame knelt and sank into the water, as at dawn and sunset, bowed to her lord and Lord, and died and Died, what might be left at the heart of her matter?

John: I wonder. Could she still rise at dawn, soar, and set with the sun?

Jane: Or would she become a lamppost rooted like Ygdrasil in rock?

John: Either way, she can light her life, her nights, or her Knight. So is she a flame or a lamppost?

(Jane does not answer.)

John *(in direct address to the audience)*: Folks, her flame is growing dim. If it goes out, she'll die. I think she could heal if children of all ages believed in prayer. If you believe, clap your hands like Deaf people do, without sound. *(He raises his hands just above his head and moves the parted fingers back and forth in synchrony, like rapid queenly waves. He moves to the front of the stage, encouraging audience members to join in Deaf applause.)* Clap BIGGER.

(Jane sees the motion in the first row and "awakens." Her gaze rises in amazement to view the audience, from front row to balcony. She is dazed and speechless.)

John: If you can't choose between life, nights, or Knight, why not choose as many as you wish?

Jane: I can pick more than one?

John: There is no law against it, and you know that already. Right?

Jane *(moon-eyed in wonder)*: Thank you for reminding me. How is it that you are always opening my eyes? *(She scans the audience and the ceiling of the theater.)* Have I dared to awaken in Ever Land? It looks so promising, this righting kinship of fish and flame.

John: A writing kinship? Right on, Jane. Think back to John 1:1: In the beginning was the Word. The Word *is* God. Righting kinship and wordplay. What a DIVINE idea. Give me five. *(He mimes slapping her hand in a high-five gesture.)*

(Jane responds in kind.)

Jane: By the way, you do know you're on fire, don't you?

John: WHAT? *(He frantically pats himself to put out invisible flames.)* I thought I smelled something burning. I thought it was you.

Jane: We've all heard of the "burning bush"—but a burning fish? That's a new one.

John: At least we'll have food while I'm dying. Wait a minute. I am not burning. Don't scare me like that. I do feel quite warm, though.

Jane: I think it's refreshingly cool in here. Maybe you're having a hot flash.

John: Very funny.

Jane: Seriously, I do see a flame all around you—the flame of kindness.

John: Where is *your* flame? *Jane, where is your flame?*

Jane: WHAT? *(She looks down in panic. She frantically pats herself to find her flame.)* I thought I smelled a stream of mountain water in spring. I thought it was you. At least we'll have water while I'm dying. Wait. I am not extinguished. Don't scare me like that. I do feel rather wet, though.

John: I'm not trying to scare you, Jane. I see a stream of life flowing through you.

Jane: Yet I feel incomplete.

(Jane and John gaze into each other's eyes, walk in a trance to meet at center stage, raise their open hands at their sides to breast level, and touch only at their hands, palm to palm, fingers to fingers.)

John: We're on the same stage. I think we're on the same page. But are we in the same painting? Do you believe in hope?

Jane: I do. Will you hope with me?

John: I will.

Jane: Do you believe in wonder?

John: I do. Will you wonder with me?

Jane: I will.

John: Do you believe in prayer?

Jane: I do. Will you pray with me?

John: I will.

(John and Jane lean toward each other and touch their foreheads together, then turn to the audience, and stand with shoulders touching.)

John *(to audience)*: If you believe in hope—

Jane *(to audience)*: — and wonder and prayer—

John and Jane *(in unison)*: —WAVE with us. *(They wave to the audience.)*

Heckler in audience: Kiss her, you fool!

(John and Jane blush and clasp hands. John kisses Jane's forehead. Curtain falls.)

The Fifth Panel

Drive nails of fear and flight into death's beast;
Claim your past, your dream, your Fate!

... Nourish always this kinship rightfully earned.

—Pleoneveia, *Somniare Perferre Canere Saltare,* lines 908-909, 912

THE MURAL

The majestic round mural, painted *sotto in sù,* extends the entire depth and width of the well-lit square back wall of a high-ceilinged gallery. At first glance through the gallery's windowed storefront, a passerby perceives the mural as a dome, which would be at a 90° angle to the wall, and wonders if the wall is actually an angled mirror. Intrigued, the passer-by retraces his or her steps to enter. The Fifth Movement of Beethoven's *Pastoral,* "Shepherd's Song—Happy, Grateful Feelings After the Storm" is playing somewhere in the gallery, not too loud, not too soft. The passerby peruses the mural's seemingly impossible scene, titled "Jane and John, names which derive from the Hebrew *Yochanan,* meaning Yahweh [The Lord] is gracious." The perimeter of the round mural is a primeval forest bordering a garden awakening with sunlight on dew. The air seems to breathe. The pi-shaped megaliths of a cromlech are placed feng-shui. Lilac and wisteria flavor the air and dip with grace over the ancient benches. Fern fronds bow and brush against the stone. Job's Tears peer out between hostas, and Stars of Bethlehem and fragrant lilies of the valley fringe the outer swath of lawn. At the rear of the garden—near the contour of the mural—violets dot iris beds amid clusters of Jacob's ladder, whose upright blue blossoms, with yellow halos and white eyes, spike outward beyond the forest contour of the mural, defying space and gravity in the *sotto in sù* scene.

In the foreground on the left, but seemingly higher than the garden in the *sotto in sù* perspective, Jane sits on a bench suspended in air, hands clasped in her lap, and smiles at her quadriptych framed in teak, supported by a central floating stone monolith that appears simultaneously distant, as though it stands far inside the wall, yet looms inexplicably gargantuan in size. On the right, directly opposite Jane, John stands with right leg forward for balance, although he's suspended in air, hands clasped behind his back. He smiles at his quadriptych framed in oil-rubbed bronze, supported by the same central monolith. On the one hand, it appears to the passerby, now an impassioned viewer, that neither Jane nor John can see each other, their sightline blocked by the distant yet massive stone. On the other hand, the *sotto in sù* perspective persuades the viewer to wonder if Jane and John are actually smiling at—maybe even flirting with—each other, or with destiny. The ambiguity is somehow pleasing, multilayered. At center front of the monolith, painted two dimensionally to appear as part of the stone, a white cat and black dog sit haunch to haunch; their mysterious sapphire and peridot eyes meet the viewer's from every possible angle. Trompe l'oeil and the cleverly skewed perspective reveal both quadriptychs to the viewer but not to the subjects in the mural. Or can they see each other and their work? The panorama of the enormous mural raises more questions in the viewer's mind.

Who *is* John really? Is he musing on memory, dream, or illusion, unaware of Jane's presence? Or are they flirting? And if so, with whom, and do they know what they are doing? Are John and Jane smiling at each other's smiles as if art and monolith have disappeared? Is this art imitating life, life imitating art, art imitating life imitating art? Which version of his fourth panel did John choose? Might a panel be missing?

Who *is* Jane really? Is Jane looking at the art for art's sake only, or an inner message, meaning in life, an ideal, a truth? Might her gaze dwell on only one of the panels? Or is she smiling at her lover? Is she loving the self or the other or both? Which version of her fourth panel did Jane choose? Might a panel be missing?

More questions may be posed, and there is no one answer. Each answer lives in the eye of the beholder.

THEIR WAY

Twilight tides through time past the Pleiades, their glimmering nebulae, the moon, luminous clouds, midnight, a moonlit quilt on a leafless landscape of winter, and wall-to-wall windows on the western side of a rural studio. John, now an elderly artist in sandals, jeans, and rolled-up sleeves, cigar in mouth, brushes strokes on an almost completed painting on canvas. Lit by wavering candlelight, Jane, now considered by most artists too elderly to model, sits nude on shimmering pewter gray silk. Her arms curve in large parentheses around her bent left leg, its foot flat on the floor, and her hands clasp gently under her other knee, a rounded V aimed at the easel. Crowning her feathered white hair, pulled back in a bun, is a small wreath twined of myrtle, white pine, and balsam, which interweave their scents in the air with the Fifth Movement of Beethoven's *Pastoral*. The circle of her wreathed and bowed head, tilted and resting at her knee, caps the parentheses of her arms. Her feet extend beyond the contour of her arms, balancing the composition: a stunning capital omega with a slipped halo. A spider spins a web over her head. At her side, a black dog, curled around a white cat, wags its tail in dream-sleep. Horses whinny from the barn out back.

John reaches for his vodka and draws blood on an exposed X-acto knife in the carrier tray.

"That's it!"

"Did you cut yourself again?" Jane calls.

He does not answer.

She rounds the easel, lets down her hair, and uses it to wipe the blood from his hand.

"Look."

On tiptoe, Jane peeks over his shoulder at the painting and gasps.

"Jane, blink once hard, open your eyes wide, and then relax. … Good."

Jane gasps again.

"I'm glad you agree, Jane."

"We deserve some champers, John."

"Yes, we do. How about some caviar, too?" He massages the small of her back. Holding a slate blue silk robe for her just so, he helps bend and slide her stiff arms into the sleeves. She turns and kneads the small of his back with her knuckles.

"When may I paint *you*, John?"

"You have seen me naked."

She leans her head into his back and laughs through the words, "Oh, John, you're still so timid after all these years."

The tease sends a shudder through him. "Sometimes it's fated, you know," he says gruffly, turning to face her.

She kisses his forehead, home to at least the third eye. "But isn't Fate grand? Without it, we'd die."

"Fate *is* death, Jane."

"If you say so." She caps the X-acto knife blade.

He grunts. "Should I think about it?"

"Let me think—what to do between now and death?"

He grunts. "Should I think about it?"

"There are no answers to some questions, John. We're all students in life."

He grunts. "Should I think about it?"

"Do I have to paint you a picture?" she teases. "And while you're waiting, let me clean that cut for you."

He does not grunt. "It's already clean."

"But—"

"Jane. Will you die with me?"

Sloe eyes adore blue respect sloe respect blue. The last note of the *Pastoral*'s Fifth Movement fades. A light snow falls in shushes outside the studio windows.

"Yes, John, I will. I will die the little death with you as often as we wish, as long as we can, up until the good death. And after that. And after that as well, at Home."

"Done," he says and kisses her forehead. "I shall pose for you tomorrow, madame."

"Some things are worth waiting for, kind sir, even if it takes a lifetime." She wraps her arm around his waist. He responds in kind, and they limp on their bad knees to the edge of the light, where they bow stiffly under a swag of black drape and merge into the mystery of night.

The First Movement of Beethoven's *Pastoral*, "Awakening of Cheerful Feelings on Arriving in the Country," scents the studio with lilac, wisteria, and hyacinth. Beyond the windows of the western wall, dawn floats at first blush, spills, and flows divine to one green pasture and one he and one she. Five daze later, Time stops … Amen.

ROISIN McLEAN writes fiction and creative nonfiction. She received her B.A. in English (both Writing & Editing, and Language & Literature) from The Pennsylvania State University, and received her MFA in Creative Writing (Fiction) from Fairleigh Dickinson University. She has been nominated four times for the Pushcart Prize and was a semifinalist for The Katherine Anne Porter Prize in Fiction (*Nimrod*/Hardman, 2006).

McLean's fiction (under various pen names) appears in or has been accepted for publication by *Perigee: Publication for the Arts, Fiction Week Literary Review, Serving House: A Journal of Literary Arts, Pithead Chapel: An Online Journal of Gutsy Narratives,* and the *FDU MFA Alumni Anthology, Inaugural Issue* (forthcoming). Her creative nonfiction appears in *Winter Tales II: Women on the Art of Aging,* in *OH SANDY! A Humorous Anthology with a Serious Purpose* (all profits of which benefit survivors of Hurricane Sandy), and in *Runnin' Around: The Serving House Book of Infidelity*. Her interviews with ex-pat author Thomas E. Kennedy appear in *The McNeese Review* and *Ecotone*.

McLean worked as Managing Editor for Macmillan Publishing Company and in hands-on book production for other publishing houses, both on staff and freelance, for over thirty years. She currently writes, revises, remodels homes, and serves as an Associate Editor for Serving House Books.